# ASSASSIN AWAKENS

## MYSTIC ASSASSIN SERIES
### BOOK ONE

THERESA CRATER

Crystal Star Publishing
1303 Alexandria St.
Lafayette, CO 80026
https://crystalstarpublishing.com

*Assassin Awakens*
Mystic Assassin Series

by Theresa Crater

Cover art by FrinaArt
Editing by Virginia King
Formatting by Polgarus Studio

Printed in the United States of America
Worldwide Electronic & Digital Rights
1st North American and UK Print Rights

This book is a work of fiction. Characters, names, places and incidents either are the product of the author's imagination or are used fictitiously, and any resemblance to any actual persons, living or dead, events, or locales is entirely coincidental.

 Formatted with Vellum

# CONTENTS

# CHAPTER
# ONE

Rainey swerved off the jogging trail and plowed straight through a mound of leaves, smiling at the memory of her mother admonishing her never to do this. You never know what might be hidden inside it, she always said. But Rainey enjoyed the rustle of fallen leaves and the earthy, musty smell that rose from the pile. She loved the occasional crunch of an acorn beneath her Nike Vaporflies. She'd never have spent that much money on a pair of shoes for herself, but they did up her game. Not that she'd admit that to Arnold. He'd given them to her on her last birthday—the only person who knew the correct date.

She reached the edge of the park and turned down the path along the river, the water deep and dark in the pre-dawn. She could just make out the yellow fans of the gingkoes that heralded the approach of full autumn. Now they were past their prime. Late October had brought hectic reds and incandescent oranges. She enjoyed D.C. this time of year, but maybe she'd pay a visit to Arnold. They could drive up into the Massachusetts mountains, check into some quaint inn, pretend to be a normal couple looking at the colors on the mountains. That is if he was in residence at The Oaks and not off on some mission.

Toward the bottom of the hill, she could just make out a figure sitting on a park bench in the gloom. She slowed a bit. He stood when she was halfway down the graveled path and walked toward her, lifting his brown trilby hat as he passed.

Maybe she'd have to put off that trip to see Arnold. Rainey paused at the bench the man had just left and bent over, putting both hands on her knees, pretending to be winded. Reaching beneath the seat, she retrieved a small plastic pouch.

She tucked it under the waistband of her running pants and resumed her route. The dark sky had turned a deep blue with just a hint of violet on the horizon. At the corner of her street, she ran flat out for the last three blocks, pushing herself. She wanted to be home before the paper-boys were out. Taking the stairs to her flat two at a time, she slipped her key into the lock and disappeared inside while her neighbors were still lost in their dreams.

Rainey threw her keys on the beat-up kitchen table, put on the kettle, and opened the pouch. Inside sat a silver thumb drive. Switching on her laptop, she double checked the security measures, then inserted the drive. One file popped up. She clicked to open it. A message swam up on the blue screen.

*Your mission, should you choose to accept it.*

"Funny," she said. Control did love his spy movies.

She waited for the rest to be decrypted.

The kettle whistled. She got up from her chair to turn it off. Outside, the sky had turned a light gray. A few delivery trucks rumbled by one street up. She rustled through the boxes of green tea on the first shelf of the cabinet and chose one mixed with lemongrass and spearmint. This one had become a favorite since her trip to Vietnam a few months ago. She spooned the loose leaves into her cast iron tea pot. She kept one at each of her hidey-holes, although she had to buy a new one more often than she liked. Filling it with boiling water, she leaned down and inhaled the aroma, letting it clear her mind.

A message now sat on her computer screen.

*The target is Charles Earl. The job needs to be completed within two weeks. Make it look like an illness.*

Rainey had been expecting this name for well over a year. Trouble was, he wasn't on her kill list.

The message disappeared and another swam into view.

*Confirm receipt*

It looked like the check-out box for on-line shopping. Rainey clicked the rectangle to verify that she'd gotten the message, then sent a quick reply.

*Final confirmation within four days.*

She took a sip of her tea and watched the screen. Control knew her protocol for accepting assignments. They'd find someone else if they were in a hurry, but the message suggested there was some leeway.

*Roger that*

*This message will **NOT** self-destruct in 5 seconds. That's your job.*

"Ha ha," Rainey said in a deadpan voice.

The message disappeared and she cleared her browsing history, then ran the security scrubber to remove all traces. She popped the thumb drive into the microwave and cooked it for two minutes. Flames danced over the drive. She left it to cool. When she went out again, she'd drop it in some random trash can.

After moving her tea and laptop to a disreputable couch

that had been green at some point in its long life, Rainey considered her target. Charles Earl had certainly aroused murderous impulses in her from time to time with his treasonous behavior and callous disregard for the law. Not to mention his sexual assaults. A recent documentary had traced his links to several Russian oligarchs whose money he laundered. Unfortunately, not enough people had watched it.

First as a candidate, then while in office, he supported dictators and alienated the country's traditional allies, allowing a foreign government to undermine democracy and the election process. So far, he'd tried to obstruct all attempts to scrutinize his crimes. His lawyers even claimed he couldn't be investigated at all. And yet with all this, he still held his position and was running a relatively successful campaign for another term. There was even a chance he'd get reelected.

Still, he wasn't on her collection of approved names.

Rainey had come back from her tour of duty in Afghanistan with a list of people she was supposed to assassinate. It didn't include individuals who she held a grudge against or necessarily the criminals involved in the continued devastation of the country where she'd almost lost her life. Even the men who had come so close to murdering her weren't on it.

When she received a name from Control that did not correspond with this list, she sought guidance. She consulted one of her spiritual advisors.

Rainey spent the rest of the morning clearing her schedule. She texted the women's martial arts academy telling them she couldn't teach the workshop they'd set up. They knew her job often called her away. They just didn't know what her job was. She'd keep her regular training appointment with Master Chu this afternoon.

Then she settled down to do some preliminary research. Earl was on the campaign trail until the election in two weeks. Great for a long-distance kill shot, but she'd have to get up close and personal to make it look like natural causes. She grimaced at the thought.

Next, she opened blueprints of the buildings he'd be speaking in and studied who would be on duty each day. After a debate in Atlanta, he was headed to his house in the Florida Keys for a Halloween extravaganza. All the top brass of the international corporations should be in attendance, plus men high in the governments involved in the ongoing conspiracy that had elected him.

His small resort and accompanying house on the private Ibis Island would accommodate his guests and security detail. This was in the two-week window. If her spiritual advisor approved the hit, it might be best to catch him there, but Atlanta was a strong contender. A presidential debate promised large crowds and lots of distractions. There would be a heavy security presence, but the chaos would afford some opportunities.

# TWO

Rainey stowed her carry-on and settled into her seat. A tall, elegant flight attendant approached immediately. Rainey asked for mineral water. She'd insisted on first class. It was a long flight and she needed to be at the top of her game. She'd do a little research and then get some sleep. Might as well not exhaust herself until the mission started.

"Here you go, Dr. Banerjee." The woman put down a napkin, then placed a brimming glass of water on top of it. "Please let me know if there's anything else I can do to make your flight more enjoyable."

She was traveling under the alias Dr. Joya Banerjee, an Indian-born biochemist. One of the advantages of her parentage was that she could pass for many ethnicities. A touch to her eyes, she was Asian. More curl to her hair, she was African American. A lilt to her voice, Indian.

"Thank you." Rainey acknowledged the courtesy with a slight smile.

"You'll find your menu in the seat pocket. We have filet

mignon, King salmon, and tagliatelle with truffles in a sherry cream sauce. I can suggest excellent wine pairings."

"I'll have the salmon for dinner," she said. "No wine."

"As you wish, madam."

An older man settled into the seat on the aisle adjacent to her. He gave her a crisp nod, then turned his attention to arranging his cubicle. Good, he wouldn't want to chat. That was another helpful thing about first class. Nobody wanted to talk. They were often too busy or too snobby.

She'd asked for the seat plus bed on the window side. Much more privacy, plus Control could afford it. Flying first class wouldn't draw undue attention. Rainey would have preferred simply slipping into the country. She didn't like being seen, but the Chinese kept a microscope on Tibet. Best to be safe with a good cover. On this trip, Dr. Banerjee consulted with a company specializing in high altitude work conditions.

Oil and gas reserves had been discovered on the Tibetan Plateau, described as a motherlode in the early twenty-first century, but the remote location and altitude posed major obstacles to its development. Early estimates for 40,000 miles of new roads and 2,500 miles of new railroad ran to three billion. Profits would repay this quickly, but the altitude was not so easy to overcome.

The plateau started at 14,500 feet, but some areas were a thousand feet higher or more. Employee fatigue was a constant problem due to the thin air. Working around explosive materials made oxygen masks impractical. The companies had developed a regime for the workers including a special diet, Tai Chi, and formerly secret Tibetan Buddhist meditations that made humans less susceptible to cold and lack of oxygen. The government denounced Tibetan Buddhism publicly, but they weren't above using it for their own purposes.

Workers were exchanged out after a three-month stint. Native Tibetans fared better, but the government insisted on sending more Chinese workers. More punishment for the rebellion. The company Rainey claimed to work for was developing a drug that would double oxygen absorption. She would collect blood samples, mail them to Control who would get them to the company under a cover story, then she'd go about her real business.

Her friend Zigsa had gotten her an audience with the current Dorje-Naljorma in three days. That should give her enough time for the flight, to collect the samples, and elude any Chinese agents who'd be assigned to follow her.

"I don't know why you have to fly to Lhasa," Control had kvetched. "The target will be in the States for the next month. The campaign is in full swing,"

"You know how I do things. You can always hire somebody else."

"Our employer wants absolute discretion, so no, I can't hire another operative."

The job should be difficult, even impossible, but it might just be doable considering how sloppy this target was, how scornful of expert advice. He'd hired private security, but the government had insisted he keep the Secret Service agents normally assigned to the White House. This meant two teams that were not well coordinated, according to Leo Strickland, the Secret Service agent assigned to the Le Clair family. Just a couple of months ago, someone had brought spy equipment into Earl's resort in Ireland. It had gone undetected for a full twenty-four hours.

Rainey opened her laptop and angled it to ensure privacy. She engaged her security protocols and reviewed his schedule for the next two weeks one more time. Her clearance allowed her to see the calendars and security details of all the candidates. If the public realized how much money all this cost, they'd shoot him themselves. She'd check out Atlanta first, but she had a hunch it would end up being the Florida Keys.

She spent the rest of her time reviewing the new Atlanta stadium, then his home, club, and his habits while in this locale. Pulling up a list of employees, she studied each person's history, then looked into the background of people in local businesses. Dinner came and she ate her salmon while continuing her research. Ibis Isle seemed to be a resort for private parties and a place for Earl to get out of the public eye from time to time.

Besides the food vendors, the business name that popped up most often in association with the resort was Pure Bliss, a massage parlor owned by a Diamond Carter. The website for the business listed a variety of treatments including hot stone massage and aromatherapy. Nothing salacious, but Rainey knew better. The pictures of the therapists seemed to be stock photos of happily smiling women in white coats. This might be a way into the resort. They'd need extra women for the party. Satisfied with her progress, she lay down in her bed. In Afghanistan, she'd learned to fall asleep under any circumstances.

Rainey had a three-hour layover in Guangzhou Baiyun International Airport. She grabbed some noodles before she boarded her next flight. This one stopped in Chongqing before finally touching down in Lhasa.

# THREE

G rant Mendez pressed his com and spoke softly. "Tycoon is on the way down."

"Roger that."

One Secret Service agent led the way, a second agent to the primary's immediate right. Grant followed behind, trying not to stare at the duck tail Tycoon's shoe-polish black hair made in the back. Maybe Elvis was his inspiration. Earl was the right age for that.

They commandeered an elevator. One of the agents produced a pass key that allowed them to ride down to the private section of the parking garage.

"Please wait here, sir," the agent in front said. He walked out, looked around, then gestured for President Charles Earl to come out.

Earl walked quickly to the waiting limo. He stuck his nose in the air, ignoring the assistance one of the Secret Service agents offered. Grant followed them to the car and started to get into the front, but Ken Doll One stopped him. "You go in the first decoy car."

The Secret Service hated the president's private security. The Red Sky team returned the sentiment, nicknaming them all Ken Doll with an appropriate number. Grant thought the name fit. Though well chiseled and quick with their reflexes, their suave ways and expensive suits made them seem like fashion dolls. Red Sky men were soldiers, tested in battle.

Grant schooled his face to show no reaction and walked up to the front limo. An identical vehicle idled behind the one Tycoon had gotten into. They mixed up the order at random.

"You get to wear the toupee." Brad Rogers held out a jet-black wig styled to look like Tycoon's hair.

"Aw, man. I wore it last time," Grant objected.

"But it looks so good on you," Brad said.

Their driver snickered.

The darkened windows of each limousine hid most of the inside from view, but just in case a shaft of light penetrated the film, somebody had to play decoy. Grant grabbed the wig and stuffed it on his head.

"It's backwards." Brad reached out to straighten the wig, but Grant slapped his hand away.

An agent tapped on the roof of their limo, and the driver pulled out into the street.

Brad had gotten him this job with Red Sky after their tour in Afghanistan. The pay was four times his old army salary and the work much easier so far. The skills he'd gained on his tour of duty were a perfect fit for this job, but the group honed those skills to a fine point. When they weren't on active assignment, they trained together, working on several forms of martial arts, weapons training, explosives, and electronics. The group offered advanced training in spy craft, counterintelligence, hacking, and computer surveillance. Whatever the person's aptitude suggested. Grant hadn't decided what to specialize in yet.

Plus, the guys hung out, drank, and caroused together. Perfected barbeque sauces in fine Carolina tradition. Hell, he didn't even mind the humidity and mosquitoes. Coastal North Carolina hosted several special ops teams and private security firms. They were a unique community who understood each other. He couldn't be happier.

Today's event was a fundraiser at a private home near Richmond. Tobacco and cotton money mostly—and these people had plenty of it. As they approached the house, Grant smirked when he saw two of those old-fashioned statues of a smiling black man welcoming guests to the house so often on display in the South. But it turned out they were real people. Two men in white outfits and red vests opened the gates. They didn't smile quite as much as the statues. His gaze darted over to Derrick, who widened his eyes in disbelief. They both quickly schooled their faces back to neutrality.

The limos drove through a tunnel of old maples, then emerged next to a mansion straight out of *Gone with the Wind*. White columns topped with crowns supported a colonnade on two stories. Black wrought-iron railings ran between the columns. An elaborate frieze topped the house. Grant found himself craving a big piece of white cake with lots of frosting.

Their car continued around the drive, passing a rounded side of the house that reminded Grant of a medieval tower, although he was sure this wasn't the proper name for it. Earl's car headed to the front of the house, and the other decoy car arrived behind them. The men hopped out and they were herded into a back room by another servant dressed in the same outfit as the men at the gate. The house buzzed with security and further in, kitchen staff rushed through two large swinging doors carrying trays of canapes.

Brad started issuing orders. "Grant, Derrick, you've got the back of the room. Watch all the doors and windows. Any sudden movements from guests. They set up the standard metal detector in front, but these old houses usually have a stash of guns."

"Roger that," Derrick said.

"George and I will be in the front."

They did a coms check before stepping into the ballroom. Small tables filled the middle and a raised platform stood at one end. An American and Confederate flag hung on the wall behind it.

Suddenly, the buzz of conversation ceased. Grant looked up to see President Earl in the doorway. He wore his usual blue suit with a red tie dangling too low in front. The lifts in his shoes didn't achieve the desired effect of making him look taller. Instead, he looked as if he'd pitch over any minute.

Earl opened his arms in a magnanimous gesture. Unfortunately, his dyed black hair paired with his paper-white skin made him look like a famished vampire inviting everyone in for a bite. Grant supposed this was close to the truth.

"Friends, friends, it is a pleasure to see you all here in this fine home." Earl started shaking hands and talking to people individually. He waded into the throng, his Secret Service detail at his side.

Grant kept his attention on the crowd in the back of the room and the various servants moving around. His gaze followed every hand reaching into a purse or pocket, every waiter reaching for a new tray. He watched facial expressions carefully. The bartender near him reached under his table and Grant moved a little closer. He stepped back when the man stood up with a fresh bottle of Scotch in his hand.

Earl stood on the podium where the head tables were set, and the host tapped on a champagne glass to get everyone's attention. Near the door that led to the kitchen, the butler whispered frantically, "Champagne trays. Hurry."

A row of young men in tuxedos filed out looking like a row of penguins. They circulated, offering trays filled with slim glasses. People grabbed them and soon the group all held their goblets of the golden liquid up.

Earl cleared his throat. "A toast to all the fine people here. We stand at a crossroads. The socialist agenda of the Democrat Party is threatening our way of life. They want to open the borders to everyone. To bankrupt the country with their free college. Most of all"—he paused and pasted a wicked grin on his face— "they want to raise our taxes and we can't have that, can we?"

The genteel crowd chuckled. A few men said in voices pitched to be heard, "Certainly not."

"So, let's keep America great." Earl raised his glass and there was polite applause. Not thunderous like his red-meat base. No shouting of campaign slogans. These people were too rich to make a racket.

Earl downed his champagne and plopped down in his chair.

Brad waved Grant forward. "Take my place behind him for a minute. I have to check on something."

The host sitting to Earl's right spoke into the president's ear. Earl nodded, then waved him to silence. He took a big bite of his steak. His potato swam in butter and sour cream, but Earl added another spoonful of both. Grant was grateful he didn't have to protect the president from his own diet. He never exercised, either.

Grant would have loved running with Clarkson. That one had kept in shape, plus he knew how to party. He had more class, too. O'Connor also jogged, but he was a saint compared to Clarkson or Butler. At least that's what the older Secret Service guys said.

Grant scanned the crowd, watching when people reached for their steak knives or put their hands under the table. He eyed the waiters bringing the red wine for the steak course.

After an hour and courses of fish and salad, then dessert, the host stood and appealed for everyone to dig deep and donate generously. "This is a defining moment in our history. Will immigrants and socialists run our country, or will we keep the reins of government firmly in our own hands where it belongs?"

Grant watched carefully as the men at the front tables reached into their pockets. They pulled out check books and started writing. Earl wiped his hands, stood, and walked to a few tables, speaking to people Grant didn't recognize, patting them on the shoulders, shaking hands. Then he headed for the door.

"Tycoon is on the move." Brad's voice sounded in his earpiece.

Grant made his way down the left side of the room, watching the people as they stood and applauded. Derrick waited by the door in the back, his gaze moving from person to person. With a nod, he followed Grant into the back hallway. They walked to the waiting limo and piled in. Derrick got the wig this time.

Brad jumped in. The Secret Service agent tapped the

roof and they pulled out, taking the middle of the group of cars this time.

"Party tonight?" Grant asked.

"Boys, we're going on a quick trip. Tycoon has been called to see the Boss."

"Man, it's too cold there," Grant objected, looking out the window at green pastures and grazing thoroughbreds.

"Nah, this time we'll be in Kosovo."

"Near the beach?" Derrick asked.

Brad gave him a withering look.

"Roger that," he said.

CHAPTER

# FOUR

A n official from the gas company met Rainey at the airport. "Dr. Banerjee, my name is Ling."

She gave him a short bow and he gestured for her to follow him through the airport and back out onto the tarmac. An Agusta A109E helicopter, excellent for high altitude, whisked her away. Once they had their headphones on, Ling explained the operation. Rainey talked enthusiastically about the research results of the drug the company was testing. She'd reviewed the protocols and biochemistry. Ever since her experience in Afghanistan, her mind was surprisingly elastic. Subjects she hadn't studied before came easily to her.

He nodded as she spoke, obviously hearing one word out of three even with the headphones, then handed over a folder complete with all the appropriate propaganda along with some actual facts.

"Thank you," Rainey said.

"Of course." The man's English was accented by way of Oxford or Cambridge.

Rainey tucked the folder into her briefcase. Ling sat

back and turned his gaze to the views. Rainey did the same, relieved she didn't have to make conversation. Helicopters were too noisy, plus she didn't relish acting. The craft cleared the clutter of the city, and the stunning peaks and green valleys unfolded beneath them, lifting Rainey's heart.

They arrived at dusk. Ling showed her to a company hotel on the edge of the facility. The place was small, but elegantly appointed. The porter took her luggage and led her up two flights of stairs, then opened the door to her room.

Two black lacquer bamboo armchairs flanked a low sofa of light gray silk. A black lacquer coffee table sat in front of it. A circle of green silk in the middle of a rectangle of mahogany decorated the wall behind the bed. On either side sat low tables and lamps with paper shades the color of butterscotch. Three lanterns with matching larger shades hung in the middle of the room. Another lacquered dresser sat to one side. Lavish for the plains of Tibet. Obviously, the site's visitors expected luxury.

The porter set her suitcase on the rack discreetly placed next to an expansive closet. She gave him five US dollars and his bow deepened. As soon as he left, she scanned the room for bugs. There were seven—three in lamps in the living room, another next to the small refrigerator and hot plate in one corner, one on either side of the bed, and a camera and listening device attached to a painting with a view of the bed. This one almost made her laugh out loud. She left them all in place.

Rainey ordered room service and poked through the folder. She'd stay off her computer until she left. The Tibetan noodles were hot and the sauce spicy. Sleep came as soon as she got into bed and she woke the next morning to a clear, blue sky.

The skin on her head felt tight and her focus off—sure signs of the thin air. She dug out a bottle of chlorophyll concentrate and downed three brilliantly green pills. She dressed in black slacks and a white blouse, threw a white lab coat over it, and filled her pant pocket with more little green pills. She'd have to be careful not to let anyone see them. After all, she was here to sell a drug to help with altitude sickness.

Downstairs, the hotel café offered American, English, and Chinese options for breakfast. She chose congee and fruit along with tea. She longed for black tea, but chose green in deference to the altitude. Too much caffeine dehydrated the body. Too bad they didn't offer coca tea here as they did in the highlands of Peru. She remembered some brew they'd given her at the nunnery while she recovered from her ordeal in Afghanistan, but she'd never gotten the names of the herbs. She'd be fine. She went up to her room and picked up a medical bag, then went downstairs.

Ling waited in the lobby. Two Chinese agents sat to the side idly reading newspapers. Ling gave her a short bow, seemingly oblivious to the presence of the agents. Or in league with them.

"I trust you slept well?"

"Yes, a wonderful room."

"Ready?" he asked.

She patted her bag. "Ready."

He headed out the door and Rainey followed him to a black Mercedes SUV. They drove the short distance to a modern steel and glass structure. The lobby offered a tribute to Mao with his picture over a fountain and a mural of happy workers all smiling in a rice paddy. Not exactly Tibet. Ling processed her through security and gave her a badge on a lanyard which she slipped over her head. He escorted her through hallways, up an elevator, and through more security into a lab.

A huddle of men in white lab coats stood around counters filled with scientific instruments.

"This is Dr. Banerjee." Ling gestured with his right arm toward the men. "Our science team." He gave a crisp bow and left.

Via a translator, Rainey explained why the company preferred to send someone to draw the blood samples rather than have the company do it themselves. "We add a new solution to the vials and it's important to get samples from a variety of workers."

The scientists nodded politely. After a few questions, Rainey set up shop. A series of Chinese and Tibetan workers paraded through, dutifully rolling up their sleeves and assuming stoic faces as she took their vitals and a blood sample. Thankfully, their medical records had already been gathered before her visit, so there was no need for any extended conversations using the interpreter.

She skipped lunch and pressed on, finishing up in mid-afternoon. The workers in the lab had spun the blood and packaged the serum for transport according to her specifications.

Ling arrived and escorted her to a fancy conference room. Rainey put on her game face and spent half an hour exuding to the top brass about the efficiency of the facility and making exaggerated promises about how the drug would extend the stamina of the workforce. The translator kept up a steady stream while men nodded and smiled. At last, they all bowed, and Rainey returned the gesture. She picked up the serum. Ling came forward to escort her back to the hotel.

"Is there any chance I could fly back to Lhasa now?" she asked. "Don't we have a few hours of daylight left?"

"Our hotel is not to your liking?" he asked.

"It's quite elegant. Lovely, in fact. I was hoping to get in a little shopping for my family tomorrow before my evening flight."

Ling eyed her package of serum.

She patted it. "It will be safe with me. No worries."

"I will check with my superior."

Ling left Rainey in the lobby under the watchful eye of Mao. He walked a few feet away and took out his cell phone. After a rapid conversation that she could not hear, he returned with a smile. "Your excursion has been approved. A guide has been appointed to take you on your shopping trip. She will know the best bargains."

"How kind," Rainey said.

*Damn,* she thought, *another person to give the slip.*

In Lhasa, a man arrived late in the night to pick up the serum. Rainey sent him off with her extra clothes and big suitcase. She kept one small bag. In the pre-dawn, she checked out of her hotel, leaving a message at the front desk for her guide that she'd received bad news from home and taken an earlier flight. Control added her name to the passenger manifest, giving her a bit of leeway to make her way through Lhasa and to the nunnery. The Chinese would figure it out soon enough and be after her, so she had no time to dawdle.

In the lobby, an agent snoozed behind yet another newspaper, easy enough to spot. Rainey went into the restaurant, which served a buffet even at this hour.

Checking that no one was around, she slipped through the service entrance and stepped out into an alley. There she threw her jacket into the garbage bin, covering it with kitchen waste. She donned a black hoodie and down jacket, shedding her identity as Dr. Joya Banerjee, and headed off.

Rainey caught a bus out of the city into the mountains, reaching the last stop by noon. She stood on the road, like all Tibetans do, waiting for a ride. Within an hour, a car sped up and stopped, letting her and an older man who'd joined her into the back seat. Providence was on her side, because the driver had a heavy foot and knew the twists and turns of the road. No one spoke English and her Tibetan consisted of a few phrases, so after saying hello and expressing her thanks, she sat back and enjoyed the view.

The car spun around the turns, coming within a hair's width of plunging into the ravine at the edge. Rainey stared down the rocky cliff, looking for wildlife. The driver looked back, surprised she had not cried out. They laughed together. Rainey wasn't concerned about dying. She'd already done it and been sent back with a job to do. It was unlikely she would get to return to that world of light until she finished it.

# FIVE

Grant stood against the wall guarding the door to the meeting area. Brad watched the opposite side of the room, shifting his weight back and forth to stay alert. They'd partied hard last night and only gotten two hours sleep. The Russians sure knew how to treat their guests. The girls had been lanky, blonde, and young. A line of cocaine had taken that dull look out of their eyes.

President Oleg Egorov sat straight, his round face neutral. "You were clear about your job, yes?" His decep-tively calm tone covered a hint of malice, but President Earl was not one to pick up on subtleties.

"I've done all that you asked. Eliminated sanctions against your country. Weakened our alliances." Earl ticked this list off on his long, skeletal fingers. "Alienated China over my talks with North Korea."

"And Iran?" Prince Burki asked, sitting back in his white thobe.

Earl shook his head in frustration. "Congress is not as easy to manage as you guys imagine. The Democrats have a majority in the house now. What about your famous algo-rithms? What happened with that election?" He glared at Egorov.

The Russian did not respond.

"You know our plans depend on US occupation of Iran. When can we expect progress on this?" Prince Burki asked.

"After this election. See what you can do about Congress," Earl growled.

A tense silence followed this remark.

"Look, I've made progress in Ukraine and with Turkey. We're close to controlling the pipelines all the way through Syria. Just a little more time and we'll have our whole plan in place."

"That will be all," Egorov commanded.

"I've done a good job," Earl objected, his voice somehow whiney and belligerent at the same time.

At a nod from the Russian leader, an assistant leaned forward and pushed a button on his laptop. The screen on one wall filled with the image of Earl naked, lying beside a boy around the age of three, also nude. The child's rear and thighs were bloodied, and he cried hysterically.

Earl hunched his shoulders. "I never—"

"I'm sure your American press will believe you. That will be all." Egorov put more emphasis on the words this time.

Earl let out a grunt as he rose from his chair. He scur-ried from the room. Brad followed, gesturing for Grant to stay.

The men remaining around the conference table waited until the sound of footsteps faded. The same assistant stood and pushed a series of buttons on his laptop. The video stopped and election projections filled the screen. "Our research predicts the candidate will lose by a margin of ten percent. We have control over returns in twenty states now. Four states are still in play."

"Democracy. How tiresome," the Prince remarked.

"Yes, your Highness," the assistant acknowledged, then continued. "Support among white men above the age of forty-five is strong, but the opposition is pulling them away with his recent speeches. Earl has not returned jobs to the former manufacturing centers and people are reacting against rising costs in food, housing, and health care. His support is soft."

"Just like his dick." Matvei Kiselev said in Russian. The other Russians in the room laughed raucously, except for President Egorov who smiled indulgently. Aside from their president, Kiselev was the richest oligarch in Russian, having earned his money first in selling off the Soviet Union's weapons arsenal, then moving on to oil. His well upholstered, corpulent form matched his wealth.

"We could change the election results if that is what you'd like," the assistant continued in English in deference to Prince Burki, "but there is a lot of attention on this type of manipulation."

"What about his running mate?" Egorov asked.

"A traditional politician. Not as compelling, but perhaps he will do," the assistant said.

"Remind me what we have on him," Egorov said.

Kiselev spoke up. "He's laundered some money for me, and his wife works for the Chinese government securing government contracts. They have large holdings in the companies involved on both sides."

Egorov nodded. "Anything else?"

"He participated in Earl's parties with under-age girls," the assistant put in. "We bought off several parents of girls they claim he raped."

Prince Burki shrugged. "I suppose the Americans care about this sort of thing, but they have not reacted to the lawsuits against Earl. I'm not sure this carries much weight with his base."

"And the Murray/Warden ticket? Have we made any progress with kompromat on them?" Egorov asked.

"Murray accepted a few bribes to get a security contract assigned to his state. That Warden is squeaky clean." The assistant shook his head in disgust.

Kiselev sneered. "I don't know how someone that naïve could make it so far in politics."

"What kind of bribes?" Prince Burki asked.

The assistant turned to his computer and a dossier on Robert Murray, the Democratic candidate for president, appeared. "Standard, really. Five million to his campaign fund for congress a few years back. Personal account in the Caymans to the tune of ten million for clearing the way for Northrop Grumman to build a mission systems factory in his state."

"No major scandals?" Egorov asked.

"Just an affair, but his wife knows about it."

Egorov shook his head. "Not promising. Let's go with our idea, shall we, Mohammad?

"Agreed." The Prince turned to their assistant. "Thank you. That will be enough."

"I do have a solution, sir," the man stammered.

"So do we. You may go."

The man bowed his head, closed his laptop, gathered his paper, and scurried from the room.

Prince Burki waited a few beats before continuing "We'll send Vasil Dushku."

"The Albanian?" Egorov asked.

"Yes."

"Excellent choice," Egorov said.

"Is the debate a good venue?" Kiselev asked.

"There will be a large audience." The Saudi prince shuffled a few papers around in front of him, apparently indifferent.

"It's decided then."

Grant wondered what they were talking about. He'd always been trained not to listen to the principals. Getting caught up in the conversation was risky. You could miss a threat. He turned his attention to the room, the posture of the men there, watched the door. But there was something going on here out of the ordinary.

"Now to more important business," the Russian president turned to his own security at the door. "Bring him in."

Grant's hand hovered above his weapon.

The security man left and in only a few minutes returned with someone Grant recognized, Daryl Forrest, former Secretary of State and head of the largest US oil conglomerate. Grant relaxed. Forrest was on the approved list.

Once he had settled at the table, a Russian assistant switched on his equipment and a map of the Arctic filled the screen. Lines in three different colors divided the area. "Melting of the polar ice caps has progressed faster than our projections. The machines that we stationed to release carbon into the atmosphere seem to have done the trick. At this rate, the area should be clear in two years."

"Excellent. At least someone is competent." Prince Burki sat back with a satisfied smile.

Egorov fixed Forrest with a hard stare. "Given our difficulties with your president's performance, your company cannot expect to keep as much of the territory as previously suggested."

Daryl Forrest sat forward in his chair, spreading both hands on the oak surface of the conference table. "Now see here, Oleg. He was your choice. We did the best we could with him, but you wanted a personality—an entertainer. That's what we delivered. You can't expect real politicians to sacrifice life-long careers to serve our interests."

"I can't?" Egorov's dark eyes bore into the oil executive. "What about the promised conflict with Iran? You have not cleaned up this little problem."

"I would hardly call it little. The American public has no appetite for another war."

"No appetite. The American public," Egorov parroted back, imitating Forrest's Texas accent. "You promised Earl could control public opinion, but you have not delivered. You will lose twenty percent of your stake."

"Twenty?" Forrest's eyes widened. "That is unacceptable."

"Twenty-five." Egorov stared him down.

Grant watched these powerful men argue and felt a surge of pride that he was charged with keeping them safe. He looked forward to Atlanta and after that, he'd heard they might get to go to the Keys. Earl physically repelled him with his emaciated body, pale complexion, and tight little mouth, but he sure did have some gorgeous women on staff. He also invited models and even younger girls to his parties. His bar was stocked with great whiskey and nicely aged Scotch. Grant was developing a taste for expensive booze. Halloween would be a wild time.

CHAPTER

# SIX

J ust before the sun set, the car Rainey hitched a ride in arrived at the drop-off for the nunnery. The driver stopped next to a wide space in the road. Rainey gave him a ten-dollar bill with her thanks. Everyone waved as the car pulled away in a spray of dust, and she began the long climb up the rough steps cut into the rock. One thousand feet above, white buildings clung to the edge of the cliff overlooking a deep ravine. Flat red roofs sporting gold pagodas came into view as she ascended.

She arrived at the top of the steps a bit winded. The porter opened the gate and spread her arms with a wide smile. "Rainey, *heb-bar kaa-su-shu.*"

She repeated the Tibetan phrase for welcome with a slight bow, hands together in front of her, then stepped into the warm embrace, feeling as if she'd come home. Or as close to it as she would get while still in this world.

Akar arrived at the gate, her maroon robes flying out behind her. "*Heb-bar kaa-su-shu.*" After a long hug, she grabbed Rainey's hand and led her to the kitchen where the gap-tooth cook handed her a large mug of herb tea.

29

The sharp taste brought Rainey fully back to the warm nest of women who had healed her, body and soul. Something unfurled inside her heart and she relaxed completely.

Footsteps sounded in the hall leading into the dining room, and Zigsa, one of the nuns who spoke fluent English, appeared. Zigsa's shining brown bob just covered her ears. Not everyone here had a bald head. She stopped in the doorframe, hands pressed against the doorframe on either side. "I see you made it, Arjuna." This was Zigsa's nickname for her.

"I did," Rainey said. "It's good to see you."

"We received your message," she said. "We are so happy to see you. You must stay at least a month, but the heavy snows will arrive after that. Then you will have to spend the winter with us."

Rainey smiled. "I may have to leave right after seeing Shenlong Yue."

Zigsa shook her head. "You have rejoined the world. Always in a rush."

"You know I would love to stay."

"Perhaps she will tell you no." A hint of disapproval at Rainey's profession crept in her voice.

Rainey shrugged her shoulders.

"We've given you your old room."

"That is very generous." Rainey wondered what memories would await her there—nightmares or the warmth of friendship.

The cook objected and Zigsa laughed. "After cook feeds you, of course."

She gestured for Rainey to follow her and they settled at the end of one of the long tables. Cook soon brought her a bowl of rice, vegetables, and lentils.

"We have repaired all the roofs from the money from that generous anonymous donor." Zigsa's eyes twinkled.

"I wonder who it could be," Rainey said with a serious face.

"As you wish." Zigsa caught her up on the community news while Rainey ate. "Choden died last February."

"I'm sorry to hear it," Rainey said.

"She was very ill."

Rainey stared down at her empty bowl. "Delicious. Thank you." The nuns ate lightly and expected the same from her.

"I believe you know the way, Arjuna. Sleep well," Zigsa said.

"*Sim-jah nahng-go*," Rainey said, the Tibetan phrase for goodnight coming easily.

Zigsa had taken to calling her Arjuna after she learned about Rainey's special assignment. She gave Rainey a well-thumbed English version of the *Bhagavad Gita*, in which the warrior Arjuna is paralyzed with doubt. He is afraid that if he kills anyone in the impending war, that he will incur bad karma. But he is equally fearful that if he shirks his duty as a warrior, he will also incur bad karma. He seeks the advice of Lord Krishna, who is serving as his charioteer. Krishan utters the famous phrase, "*Yogastah kuru karmani*."

Rainey read the book straight through and assailed her friend with questions at breakfast the next morning. "*Yogastah kuru karmani*. What does that even mean?"

"Established in Being, perform action."

Rainey spread her hands in a gesture of impatience. "Can you explain more?"

"It means to gain enlightenment, to rest the mind in Absolute Consciousness, and from that place right action will spontaneously occur. You will always be in dharma."

31

"Great. I'll just pop into enlightenment."

Zigsa smiled.

"And dharma is?" Rainey asked.

"Right action. The job you were sent here to do in this lifetime."

Rainey snorted.

Zigsa pointed a finger at her. "And you, my friend, are lucky. You were told directly by the divine force what you were sent back to do."

Rainey stared at her.

Now smiling at the memory of how she'd received this nickname, Rainey got up from the table. After dropping her plate and cutlery in the kitchen, she lit a butter lamp and made her way to her old room, taking her time. Her feet remembered the uneven floors and the creaky stairs. The windows framed in golden wood looked out at the mountains, but the sun had gone down. The Milky Way adorned the night sky with a luminous glow.

Rainey stuffed her pack into a cubby hole, tracing the familiar shelf with her hand. The room itself was only just larger than a closet. The glow of the lamp light softened the brilliant blue, yellow, red and gold paint on the walls and furniture. Tibetan houses, even nunneries, looked dull on the outside, but inside they were a riot of color.

Rainey stood in front of a painting of Green Tara on the wall. "Hello again." She traced the goddesses features with her finger. She supposed she should prefer Black Tara, who took revenge, but she'd healed with this figure watching over her.

She made her way up to a communal bathroom that the head of the nunnery had installed recently with money from the same anonymous donor. "The modern world has brought us a few good things," the Dorje had said. Rainey washed away the dust and sweat from her journey. She pulled a long cotton tee-shirt over her head, returned to her cubby hole, and crawled under the quilt in the narrow bed against the wall. Listening to the quiet rustling of night birds and small mammals in the bushes outside, Rainey nestled down onto the familiar lumpy mat and fell asleep.

# CHAPTER
# SEVEN

The sound of chanting wove into her dreams and gently woke her. Oh, no. She'd wanted to show up for the pre-dawn meditation. She started to jump up, but decided not to disturb the nuns with her late arrival. Instead, she lay in bed, letting the complex harmonies swirl around her and sink into her muscles and bones. She remembered how she'd lay here, too injured to make her way to the morning rituals. Then later, how she'd listened, too heart sick to join her new sisters. It had taken her time, but she'd finally healed and then fully remembered her experience on the other side through the patient guidance of the head of the nunnery, the current Dorje-Naljorma, and the seer Shenlong Yue.

After the pre-dawn chanting stopped, Rainey shrugged off the quilt. The chill mountain air brought goosebumps on her arms and legs. She dressed quickly and went down to the dining room. No one else was there, so she made herself a cup of tea and sat in her favorite corner watching the snow-capped peaks blush under the rising sun.

Zigsa arrived in the dining hall and waved Rainey over. "The Dorje-Naljorma can see you now," she said in a soft voice.

Rainey followed her friend to the door of formal meditation room, where Zigsa stopped and gestured for Rainey to enter. The current Dorje-Naljorma sat on a raised rostrum at the end of a long hall. Mats where nuns sat to perform the daily rituals and scheduled meditations ran the length of the room forming a central corridor. A few nuns remained. Rainey put her hands together in a formal greeting, bowed at the waist, then made her way past the mats. They nodded to her as she passed. When she reached the rostrum, she bowed again.

An old claw of a hand reached out, grasped Rainey's chin, and lifted her face. The Dorje smiled, her eyes almost disappearing in the wrinkled face. "Dear daughter, you have returned. You bring happiness to my heart each time you come home."

Rainey's eyes filled. "It is good to see you."

"What brings you to us this time?"

"A name."

"Ah, you must see Shenlong Yue. It is not for me to deal in death." Her voice was light, not passing judgment.

Much to her surprise, Rainey had discovered the older Buddhists viewed her profession with equanimity. Death was a transition as was birth. It was not for them to judge anyone's actions. The not judging part was something Rainey was far from mastering.

"Now tell me, how is your meditation?"

Rainey spent the next half hour talking about her spiritual practice, getting advice about a few problems. She talked about her life and her new martial arts instructor,

Master Chu. She even found herself telling her teacher about Arnold.

"A man in your life." The Dorje's eyes sparkled. "You have healed."

Suddenly shy, Rainey looked down at her lap.

"I am well pleased with you, my daughter."

Rainey met her spiritual mother's eyes again. The Dorje chucked her under the chin just like a baby, making Rainey laugh. Then the Dorje turned serious and gave her a thorough blessing complete with chanting and the application of an unguent oil over her third eye.

Once she was done, the Dorje nodded. "Shenlong will be waiting for you."

Rainey stood, but before she turned to leave, the Dorje said, "You don't have to have a name to come and visit."

Rainey's heart softened and she bowed. "Yes, Mother."

Zigsa escorted her down a series of passages, up some rickety stairs, and down another hallway without speaking. Rainey appreciated the time to compose herself before her audience with Shenlong Yue. The seer was a Chinese woman who'd been given asylum here and decided to stay.

At the end of the hallway stood blue doors carved with elaborate Chinese dragons on each side. Zigsa knocked three times and waited. A bell sounded and she opened the door, giving Rainey's arm a squeeze before she put her palms together in the more formal sign for namaste. She bowed her head slightly. Rainey returned the gesture, took a deep breath, and walked into the darkened room. Even though Shenlong was a friend to both of them, one never knew what she'd be like when she was speaking for the other worlds.

Red silk banners hung from the walls with gold circles down the middle depicting Chinese characters. Rainey had never learned what they meant. Incense rose in clouds from two tall bronze burners on either side of an elaborate screen featuring a twisting scarlet dragon.

A buzzing sound came from behind the screen, then a gravelly voice asked a question in Mandarin. It was the most commonly spoken dialect, one that Rainey had studied in her black ops training. "What do you want from the Spiritual Dragon?"

"I have come to ask a question of life or death, Honored One," she answered in the same language.

Wooden slats in the middle of the screen moved slightly and an eye appeared. "It is you." This time Shenlong's voice was normal.

"Hello, my friend."

"I heard a rumor you were here."

"The rumor is true. It is good to see you," she said once again.

"You as well. How can I help?"

"I have a name that is not on my list."

After a sharp intake of breath, the slats snapped closed. Shenlong began to pray. It was one she had taught to Rainey during her convalescence, so she joined in. They asked for a clear connection and divine guidance, giving thanks as if they'd already received it.

"What is the name?" Shenlong whispered.

Rainey leaned forward and said quietly, "Charles Jefferson Earl."

Then there was silence.

It was unlikely Shenlong recognized the name. She'd given up on the outside world once she entered this sanctuary and didn't follow the news. Shenlong fell silent as she consulted her guides.

Rainey settled back on the cushion in front of the dais

to wait. Shenlong Yue had shared her own story one night as they sat out under the river of light that was the Milky Way. Rainey had known her time to leave the nunnery was near. She'd healed physically, but more importantly had gained an understanding about what had happened to her. The two friends sat together enjoying a last evening together.

Shenlong broke their long, companionable silence. "I know something of what you've experienced."

Rainey turned to her, seeing only the dim outline of her face in the dark. "Tell me if you wish."

After a moment, Shenlong began. "It was during the cultural revolution. The Red Guard was purging what they called 'impure' elements from society. My family had been wealthy before the revolution. My great grandfather served the emperor." Her voice rose in what was almost pride.

"He was killed because of this. The family escaped. My parents worked the fields for a long time, but because we had experience governing, my father was approached. He joined the party—everyone had to—and worked in our region. When the Guard arrived in our house, they killed our parents in front of us, arrested my brother, and dragged me off. I never made it to prison. At fourteen, I was like a newly budding lotus."

"I'm so sorry," Rainey said.

"They turned me over to the head of the Guard who used me as his concubine until he tired of me. Then he gave me to his men."

Rainey reached out and took Shenlong's hand, giving it a squeeze. From below, a nightjar called out.

Shenlong took a shuddering breath. "They had me for three days before they threw me on the village garbage heap, thinking me close to death. I wanted to die."

Rainey nodded in the darkness and her friend seemed to sense it.

"While I was unconscious, Quan Yin appeared to me. She said she would give me a gift. I begged her to take me. I didn't want to come back."

"I know," Rainey said.

"She held me in her arms all night, singing to me. When I woke up, I was in an old widow's home. She was singing the same song Quan Yin had sung. Perhaps it was the widow all along."

"Perhaps." Rainey tone suggested they both knew better.

"This woman nursed me back to health. One night she asked me what she should do to stay safe and that's when I discovered Quan Yin's gift. The Wind Dragon spoke through me, prophesizing the woman's daughter would return with a grandchild. When it was time for me to leave, the Wind Dragon showed me an image of this place and told me I would be welcomed here."

"How long did it take you to find it?"

"Oh, two or three months traveling by night. A few times I was able to get a ride in cars or wagons."

"Did they—"

"Never again. I could always tell who was safe to travel with."

"Good," Rainey said.

"You will be safe as well, my friend."

They were silent for a while. "But I have not been granted the gift of prophecy," Rainey said.

"No, but you will make the world safer. It is an honorable profession."

The rustle of silk brought Rainey back to the present. The wooden slats in the dragon screen snapped open.

Movement came from behind the screen as Shenlong Yue slid closer to give her pronouncement, but it was the gravelly voice of the Wind Dragon that spoke. "It is ordained."

Rainey sat back on her heels. She thought that meant the mission was a go, but had just a sliver of doubt.

Then Shenlong's normal voice whispered, "You have permission, Arjuna."

CHAPTER
# EIGHT

R ainey reached Lhasa that evening and slipped into a busy teahouse near Danjielin Temple. With a nod to the proprietor, she headed to the washroom and rinsed off the road dust. At her preferred corner table in the back, a waiter arrived with her favorite noodle dish which she quickly devoured. Satisfied, she sat back with a large mug of sweet chai to catch up on the news and location of her now-approved target.

With just over a week to go, Earl had been campaigning, hitting cities in Pennsylvania and Michigan. His die-hard fans still turned out and chanted insults against his opponent from four years ago or the new one against members of Congress. The media ridiculed them, but rung their hands over his poll numbers. Ten points behind the Murray/Warden ticket, but after 2016, nobody was taking anything for granted.

The propaganda station reported him to be fifteen points ahead. Word was he'd fired the last pollsters in his campaign who'd reported anything close to the truth to him. At least he hadn't executed them like Kim Jong-Un, who'd killed the negotiating team he'd sent to South Korea.

Earl was due at the debate in Atlanta in two days, but had returned to the White House. Rainey accessed his secure schedule, but no meetings popped up. She thought he must be recuperating. With the impeachment vote in the House of Representatives and the trial in the Senate, Earl had gotten increasingly erratic.

A surge of fury heated her stomach. The spineless House leaders had hemmed and hawed before finally issuing subpoenas for a series of witnesses. They'd had to take each name through the courts and serious hearings had begun only three months ago. Now in the Senate, the compelling testimony got lost in the noise of the campaign and only the most politically savvy Americans followed it. Gutless cowards. They'd left it for her to clean up.

Rainey sat back in her chair and made herself focus on her breathing until the fire in her solar plexus reduced to a warm glow. She had a job to do, a job she'd been appointed to, one she'd come to accept. When Zigsa gave her a copy of the *Bhagavad Gita* while she was recuperating at the nunnery, she suggested that Rainey, like Arjuna, should accept her destiny.

She focused back on the task at hand and made a decision. Atlanta—she'd go to Atlanta and observe, then make her way to his resort in the Keys. She sent an encrypted message to her Secret Service contact asking when Earl would arrive and where he'd be staying, then closed down her electronics.

She finished her chai and left a big tip on the table. Making her way through the kitchen, alive with the bang of pots and pans, the smells of ginger and lemongrass, she went into the back hallway. She climbed the narrow steps to the second floor and walked to a storeroom in the back. Checking to be sure she was unobserved, Rainey closed the door and locked it. Then she moved boxes of tea and other spices that were stacked against the wall. Once the wall was clear, she pushed a panel. It released easily.

Rainey pulled out a metal box from the hidden space, dialed in the combination, and opened the lid. Shuffling through a few passports, she decided on the identity of Mia Woods—young, rich, searching for herself or a good distraction. She took a stack of American dollars.

While she was at it, she checked the weapons stash. The Glock 19 and the smaller Ruger LCP were freshly oiled. Mipam Tashi, who owned the shop and worked in the Tibetan resistance, took good care of her stockpile. She left the weapons, but took a small knife made of a hard plastic that would not set off the alarms.

She stuffed five hundred dollars into an envelope for Mipam, then donned a baseball cap with an embroidered symbol for Shiva on the front and headed out. On the streets, the weather had turned cold with tiny pellets of hail falling. Rainey walked to a boutique in a fancy hotel where she bought a few outfits that fit Mia's profile. In a separate store, she procured a new suitcase. In yet a third shop, she bought make up, then headed to the airport.

Control's hacker 7R4C3R kept up a convincing social media presence for Mia. Rainey reviewed the Facebook and Twitter account to see what Mia had been up to lately. Apparently, she'd been in New York at some art openings, then gone off to Hong Kong to attend a lecture from a noted Buddhist monk. Rainey had to hand it to 7R4C3R. It had taken her forever to realize this acronym stood for Tracer. His real name was anybody's guess.

In the ladies' room in the airport lobby, Rainey slipped

on the personality of Mia Woods along with the makeup and change of clothes. She flounced up to the ticket counter, plunked down an American Express card, and purchased a ticket for the evening flight to New York with a connection to Atlanta. She rattled on in a breathless voice about how she just loved Tibet. "Those maroon robes. And the chanting." She pressed her hand to her chest and closed her eyes. "Enthralling."

"Yes, ma'am. Will you be checking any luggage?" The clerk eyed Rainey's dress and hat as if she were expecting three cases.

"Just the one." She held out her hand for her boarding pass.

"Gate eight. Have a good flight."

Mia settled into business class and turned on a series of movies which she largely ignored. When she landed in New York, she had a message from John Morton, her contact in the Secret Service.

*Call me when you land.*

After clearing customs, Rainey almost missed her new suitcase. Yes, it was the bright pink one. Just what Mia would pick. She wheeled the atrocity off to an empty hall and phoned John. It took almost a full minute before he answered.

"Where are you?" came his quiet voice.

"I just landed at Kennedy."

"The Skeleton is in Pristina meeting with his handlers." They'd given Earl this unofficial code name. "We'll be in Atlanta tomorrow. Can you give the stadium a once-over for me? See where our holes are?"

Rainey waited for a couple to walk by, then said, "Sure thing."

"I appreciate it."

"He'll be at the Ritz?"

"Always."

"See you there."

"Not if I see you first."

Morton clicked off before she could offer a comeback.

Rainey grabbed her luggage and ran to catch her Atlanta connection. She wanted to leave the pink monstrosity, but it would get picked up by security and traced back to Mia Woods. She couldn't put that identity at risk or draw any attention to her travel.

# CHAPTER
# NINE

Rainey parked near the Mercedes-Benz Stadium in Atlanta, skirted past an empty ticket booth, and made her way across the parking lot. She spotted the employee entrance. Workers flashed their badges. Outside, a food truck sold coffee and breakfast sandwiches. She joined the line. A large man in a blue work shirt stood in front of her. In front of him, a woman gossiped on her phone.

"Girl, you know it. We was at the club until three o'clock." She listened, then laughed. "Yeah, I wanted to call in sick, but I done it too many times already."

The woman's employee badge peeked out of the back pocket of her tight jeans. The man in the blue shirt turned to wave at a friend and Rainey reached around him and gently drew the ID out of the woman's pocket. The picture didn't match. The woman was darker than Rainey and had quite elaborate braids, but in her experience, people checking badges rarely looked at them closely.

Rainey got out of line and walked behind a group of people headed for the door who were chatting among themselves. She nodded occasionally and laughed when they did. She flashed her badge and the attendant waved her through. Very lax for a presidential event.

Rainey snagged an orange vest, hung the ID so the picture was against her shirt, and walked down to the floor of the stadium. The football field had already been covered up and chairs were being put out in rows. She stared up at the dome. She'd studied the building online. When closed, the roof resembled a filigree flower with eight elaborate panels. On the outside, the closed dome sported the company logo, but the rest of the building continued the flower motif with eight petals on top and eight large sides folded over like larger petals. It reminded Rainey of Japanese origami.

Last night when she'd driven by, the lights trained on the building turned the sides into illuminated pyramids. Pretty place. Fit more for a party convention than the final presidential debate, but Earl had a flair for the dramatic.

"You gonna just stand there?" The man pointed to the cart full of chairs.

Grabbing a handful, Rainey started unfolding them, then lining them up. When she got to the end of a row, she muttered, "Bathroom," and headed off. She walked the perimeter. Teams of security in black walked the halls, some carrying the Glock 9mm that identified them as Secret Service. Others, dressed identically, carried Berettas. So Cobra Squad was here. Probably Red Sky as well. She wondered what other corporate or black ops teams wandered these halls.

The concessions and food stands bustled with people cleaning countertops and tables, unpacking boxes, stuffing refrigerators in the back, ready to do big business. Some restaurants offered a full view of the floor. In others, full screens kept the customers apprised of the game in progress. During the debate, these would feature close ups of the candidates. Between the cluster of restaurants, booths selling political buttons, bumper stickers, hats, and t-shirts had replaced the stores that usually sold team paraphernalia.

Making a full round, she checked out the lobby where a shout went up just before the large Atlanta Falcons banner fluttered to the ground to be replaced by one with Earl's smug face. The two parties had tables on opposite sides of the lobby. A cluster of people in blue t-shirts sporting Murray's face listened to a woman giving orders.

A bored security guard stood next to the stairs to the next floor. She waited a while, pretending to study her phone. Finally, a young woman stopped to ask him for directions, and he walked a few steps with her. Rainey slipped up the stairs to check the luxury boxes.

These halls were virtually empty. She looked into the corporate and privately-owned boxes, taking in the lay of the place. They overlooked the arena. Lots of dangerous possibilities here.

Up another level, she retrieved the picks from a hidden pocket in her backpack and made quick work of the locks of the utility rooms, starting with the one nearest the stairs. She checked the lighting and computer banks. All quiet. Nothing strange on the floor. No unusual cables. She pried open the door to the catwalks and scanned.

The door to the next room was unlocked. Rainey eased the door open and looked inside. It seemed like the other utility room, a panel of switches to one side, electrical cords rolled up and stashed. Boxes of bulbs were stacked on the other side. She moved one box on the end and spotted a duffle bag behind it. She waited, listening for any sound.

Voices rose up from the coliseum below. No distinct words made it all the way up to her, just a dim background to the quiet buzz of the electrical panel. Certain she was alone, Rainey made her way over to the duffle bag. She crouched down and unzipped it. Inside was a folded tripod. Beneath that, something else. The fitting for a sniper rifle.

A chill ran through her. Neither the Secret Service or Cobra Squad would put a shooter up in the rafters of the stadium. Maybe they'd station lookouts up here, but nobody with a rifle like this.

Rainey found an access door to the skywalks leading to the equipment and lights near the ceiling and picked the lock. She walked out on one, crouching low, her steps silent. Far below, tiny workers scurried around preparing the seating in the playing field in front of the stage. If she fell, she'd splatter all over the floor. She made her way to the end of one catwalk, then stepped over a railing and balanced on the metal tightrope that lead to a group of lights.

Just behind them, the support beam widened to make a space large enough for the tripod, attached gun, and a shooter. She looked between the two spotlights in front of the space. They framed the stage perfectly. Taking a scope out of her pack and holding it up to her eye, she focused on the space below. The target would be right there, perfectly lit—a sitting duck.

Whoever this assassin was, he had no intention of making this hit look like an accident. He planned to shoot him on stage in the middle of the debate with millions of people watching. Her assignment was to make Earl's death look natural.

But what if they were after Murray? The set up suggested the nearer podium was the target and that was

Earl's. Still, she had to consider all the possibilities. She'd have to stop this plot.

Was there a place where the sniper would be a sitting duck? Not that she wanted to shoot the person, but if she took the tripod, the shooter would know they'd been discovered. Still, best to start with the last resort to stop the plot and work her way back.

Rainey glanced around, looking for a matching spot with a straight line of sight to this place. Huge spotlights like the ones she sat behind hung at regular intervals across the ceiling, eventually forming a circle. She looked for a visible platform. She found two locations that seemed likely candidates.

She counted the struts between her current perch and the first possibility, then made her way carefully back to the utility room and brought up the blueprint of the building on her phone. Finding the area, she noted the numbers of the rooms that most likely gave access to the set of lights she wanted. She stashed her equipment in her small pack and opened the door. Checking that the hall outside was still empty, she set off.

Rounding the curve of the hallway, she heard the scrape of a door ahead of her opening. She came to a small alcove with a trash can and ducked behind it. Quiet steps approached. She controlled her breathing. A small gap between the wall and the container showed a sliver of the hall. A man walked by dressed in black. He carried another duffle bag, a match to the one she'd found.

Rainey caught a glimpse of the man's face. She recognized him instantly. Vasil Dushku. Known by most as the Albanian.

The infamous assassin.

Good thing he was on her list.

Reaching to the small of her back on instinct, Rainey found nothing. She'd left her weapons in the hotel room, except for the thick plastic knife that didn't set off the metal detector. She pulled it from her boot and crept out from behind the garbage bin.

She tiptoed down the hall, not making a sound, and saw Dushku stop in front of the door to the utility room where Rainey had found the tripod. He opened the door and disappeared inside.

Rainey decided against following him. She only had her knife. She might be able to take him with just her fighting skills, but he was most likely armed. Besides, the Albanian was a legend.

Dushku had been the head of intelligence under Berisha and been charged with torture. Not just ordinary torture, either. The stuff he did made her sick to her stomach. When Berisha was deposed, Dushku had escaped the country before being apprehended. Finally arrested in London in 2012 where he'd been living under a false name, he escaped again and word had it he established a black ops group somewhere in the Mediterranean where he took contracts, doing extreme interrogation, assassinations, and gun running. The CIA and MI6 had tried for years to locate him, or so they said. Seeing him here, Rainey wondered if they'd known his location all along and used him for contract work.

She jogged back the way she'd come, heading for the stairs, then remembered the security guard down below. She slowed to a walk, took out her employee ID, and waved it at the security screen to the elevator, praying the woman she'd stolen it from had clearance for this section. The gears engaged and Rainey heard the car rising.

She took out her phone and studied it, keeping her head

tucked down and face to the elevator doors. The scrape of a door down the hall tied knots in her stomach.

The door to the elevator opened. She stepped inside and without turning around, hit the button for the lobby.

Someone was running down the hallway. She pushed the button to close the door. It didn't respond. She started punching her phone, pretending to be distracted by a text message. The footsteps continued and Rainey glanced out of the side of her eye. The doors slid closed before the person reached it, and she breathed a sigh of relief.

In the lobby, Rainey tossed her orange vest in a garbage bin. On her way out, she grabbed a Murray t-shirt from a pile and pulled it over her head. It was too big, but that helped to disguise her more. Outside, she passed the huge metal falcon in the front of the coliseum. Federal security officers had started setting up barriers on the roads into the stadium. Rainey turned down a side street and stopped behind a sugar maple. She had a good view of the parking lot, but after an hour, she hadn't seen Dushku again. Either he was still inside or had left in a different direction.

The swarm of humans getting ready for their campaign activities increased along with the presence of security. The metal barrier surrounding the whole area was almost complete. The best option would be to stop Dushku the night of the debate. She knew his plan. Even if he changed location, she'd have to find him. Maybe she could get to him before he got out on the beam with his rifle.

She slipped through a few backyards. She scaled a wooden fence and a pit bull took exception to her presence. Standing stock still, she calmed her breathing and started to hum a Tibetan mantra. The dog growled, then cocked his head and settled to the ground.

"Good boy," she said.

The dog gave a tentative wag.

She crouched down and scratched him behind his ears. "Sorry I don't have a treat."

She walked slowly to the other side of the yard, scaled the fence, and made her way to the truck she'd borrowed at the airport. She planned on returning it with a full tank of gas. Driving off, she kept careful watch that she wasn't being tailed. She pulled out and passed a few cars parked on the road. No vehicles followed. Staying alert, she took some false routes, but saw nothing. Of course, the Albanian was one of the best. He still might be there somewhere. Invisible.

Once she was reasonably certain she wasn't being followed, she returned to her room and updated Control on developments. He sent her the address for the new location of their weapons master in Atlanta.

Then she put in a call to Morton.

"You in Atlanta?" he asked without preamble.

"I am."

"Good. Been to the coliseum yet?"

"That's what I'm calling about."

Morton's chuckle warmed her ear. "What's your report?"

"Two words. The Albanian."

"Fuck."

"Yeah, you've got trouble."

"What's he up to?"

"He's planning on shooting Earl during the debate. Big audience. Huge media coverage."

"Where's he set up?"

"Right now, behind one of the big spotlights in the ceiling. But he knows somebody was up on that floor. He may move."

"Think he'll go to another spot in the ceiling?"

"Maybe. Or he'll find somewhere else. But I think he'll stay up high. He's got a sniper rifle fitted with a scope."

"You should stay in the Ritz where I can protect you."

Morton's concern warmed the cold pit in Rainey's stomach. This was one of the world's most dangerous killers, after all, but her fear came mostly from his creativity as a torturer. "Can't. I'll lose my anonymity."

"You sure?"

"I'll be careful."

CHAPTER

# TEN

Dushku heard the doors to the elevator close. Someone had been up here. When he unlocked the utility room this morning, everything had been as he left it. He'd gone down to get the rest of his equipment, but been delayed by the extra security. Now he noticed the duffle bag had been disturbed. He'd placed a small length of transparent plastic cord across the zipper. Very thin. Nothing anyone would notice. It was gone. He got on his hands and knees and searched, and found it across the room. Someone had moved his bag. And worse, probably opened it.

He stepped out into the hall and spotted someone in an orange vest getting into the elevator. Male or female, he couldn't tell. He ran down the corridor, but the doors closed before he could see who it had been. A worker? Probably not. The person moved like a martial artist, not some sloppy temp hired to do manual labor getting the place ready for the debate. But the figure had been slight. Maybe a woman? Probably not. This job required fighting, not seduction or misdirection. At any rate, a spy. Operatives forgot to slouch, to drag their feet when they walked. Their body language always gave them away.

Dushku made his way back to the utility room. The top floor was empty except for occasional security teams that he could easily elude. He gathered the duffle bag containing the tripod and searched for the room he'd marked as his second choice. He picked the lock and set down the bag. Opened the door to the catwalks and made his way to the bank of lights. Same wide section behind them. He double checked the view. It would do. Next, he unpacked the rest of the equipment he'd brought today, stashed it behind a row of boxes, relocked the door to the utility room, and went back to his hotel. On the way, he picked up a packaged sandwich from a 7-11.

Back at the Country Guesthouse—a rather fanciful name for a low-rent hotel in the middle of the city in his opinion, but it was anonymous—he switched on his computer, accessed the SVR server, and searched for known assassins and their current location. This would take a few minutes.

Running a pen knife through the plastic wrap sealing his sandwich, he took it out. Roast beef on white bread and dry at the edges. He considered the small packages of mayo and mustard, then threw them in the trash. He took a bottle of Brauhaus Bockbier from the small fridge and opened it. What a surprise to find a beer from home. He'd bought a case of it. The beer washed the dry bread down.

Lighting a cigarette, he went to the window and watched trash blow around in the parking lot. The computer dinged. He crushed out the cigarette, tossed the butt outside, and sat in front of the screen, running his eyes down the list. Nobody anywhere near Atlanta.

He pulled up Earl's schedule. He was due in the Keys

right before the election. Dushku looked for anyone in Florida or the Caribbean.

Nothing.

He picked up his phone and called the only number in it.

"Joe's Pizza."

"I'd like to order a pepperoni with anchovies. Extra cheese."

"Hold, please."

After a series of beeps, a familiar voice came on the line. "Dushku. This is unexpected."

"Another sniper has the same assignment."

"What?"

"Somebody was snooping on the ceiling catwalks. They got out before I could ID them."

"Are you certain this is an assassin?" Kiselev finally asked. "Not just a routine check by the Secret Service or one of the private security groups?"

"He discovered my tripod and left it. Have you seen any alerts on the agency sites?"

"Nothing."

"If nothing is reported in the next two hours, then I have competition."

"Hmm." Clearly, Kiselev had his doubts. "Should we just let him do the job? You be ready if he fails?"

"*Nyet*," Dushku shouted, insulted by the suggestion. "We know nothing of his plans. Don't you want a show? To make a martyr of him? This I can do like no other."

"All right, Dushku, calm down. I'll put another man on him. You stay focused on the primary target."

"As you wish."

Dushku ended the call and crushed out another half-smoked cigarette. He wouldn't follow Kiselev's orders. He didn't want some amateur messing up his plans.

He took out his sniper rifle and started cleaning it. The routine calmed him, helped him think. Then he moved on to his MSS *Vul*, a silent pistol. He needed them both well oiled, in tiptop shape for tomorrow.

Now, how could he find this mystery assassin?

# ELEVEN

The presidential entourage had one more campaign stop before the last debate, and Grant had the dubious honor of riding in the limo with Earl. The man talked incessantly.

"Moron Murray. What a loser," he shouted to nobody in particular. "He's way behind." He looked around for agreement.

"Yes, sir," one of the Ken Dolls responded, but not with enough enthusiasm to satisfy Earl.

"The polls are a hoax."

Another man nodded.

"It's true. They're all frauds. Every one of them," Earl said, increasing his volume.

"Yes, sir," the two Ken Dolls shouted.

Somewhat mollified, Earl started mumbling about the impeachment by the House Judiciary Committee. "Sniveling Snyder. Trying to dig up dirt on the President of the United States with that committee of his. They made it all up. He's a fucking traitor." His face turned a deeper red.

Earlier in this assignment, Grant would have been

puzzled by these comments considering the meeting with the Russian president and Saudi prince they'd just come from, but he'd stopped trying to figure the guy out. One thing he had finally realized, though. Earl would talk until he convinced himself. He supposed it was a form of self-hypnosis, although he wasn't really sure what that term meant.

Earl grabbed his phone and started tweeting. He would probably type out everything he'd just said, and they'd all have to hear it all over again on the news. Except Grant didn't listen to the news much. When they'd gotten back from Kosovo, he'd caught a glimpse of a report on the screen at the airport. There had been another mass shooting, this one a gay club in Springford, Connecticut.

The news anchors were talking about the man's online posts. They were examining his mental health. Before Earl could see the news, one of the Secret Service agents turned the channel to his favorite propaganda station. But Earl had been briefed about it on the plane. The press would be sticking their microphones in his face when they caught up with him, expecting a sane statement.

*Good luck with that*, Grant thought.

On the plane to South Carolina, Brad told him that Earl had sat in a depressed heap after President Egorov reamed him a new one. He'd finally roused himself after he heard about the shooting, shouting about how immigrants were destroying his presidency. The shooter was white, as far as Grant knew. Plus, what did immigrants have to do with fags—or the LGBTQ community, he was supposed to say.

*Fuck all those letters.*

They pulled into the underground parking for the Star Sports Center in Greenville. Earl hadn't gotten any rest on the plane and had been ranting the whole limo drive. Grant wondered if he'd have the energy to yell some more, but his base was eager for red meat.

The Ken Dolls and local police ushered Earl into a lavish green room where the South Carolina senator started the shoulder pounding. A line of other people probably running for state office formed up to be introduced. One of the Ken Dolls said that Senator Dickenson's polls were as dismal as Earl's, but Grant figured the senator was looking to turn that all around with this magic rally.

Brad rushed into the room and started issuing orders. "Grant, Derrick, stage left. Walk the aisles. George and I will take the right side."

"Roger that."

Grant and Derrick slipped out a small door under the stage and took up their positions. The restless crowd waved their signs at the cameras, yelling "Bogus news" and "Shoot the press!"

Grant started looking for guns. For once, he was glad of the Ken Dolls and even the local yokel backup. He lost track of time, absorbed by the fast movements and loud shouts of the crowd. Local officials came out and the group quieted down a bit, bored and waiting for the main event.

Derrick strode up to him. "See anything?"

"Nah, but it's hard to tell," Grant said.

"Too much going on."

While the crowd mostly sat, Derrick and Grant walked in opposite directions. Most wore blue jeans and big t-shirts that covered their waists, making it a bit hard to check for a bulge in the mid-back. The audience had gone through two metal detectors to get inside, but still, this was their job. Many wore campaign hats and hostile expressions.

"What you lookin' at?" A man suddenly jumped up and

pressed his weather-beaten face close to Grant's, taking him by surprise. "Huh? You ain't never seen a patriot before?"

Grant took a step back.

The man closed the gap with another step. "I asked you a question." His breath smelled of cigarettes and hot dogs.

One of the local police moved up. "Is there a problem, sir?" He addressed himself to Grant.

But the redneck spoke up. "Yeah, this wetback's staring at my wife. Fuckin' immigrants."

"Actually, he's working with us tonight, sir," the officer replied, keeping his voice calm, even cheerful. "Helping to keep our president safe."

"Sheeeit." The man hawked up a wad of spit, then remembered where he was and swallowed.

Grant's stomach twisted.

The patriot turned to the cop. "You should hire some real Americans, sir." He spat out this last word, but returned to his seat.

"Thank you," Grant said to the policeman.

"Any time." The officer took a solid stance next to the redneck's row, hands folded in front of him.

Grant never really thought of himself as Latin until he visited his family, and even then, they were just his parents and siblings, their husbands and wives, their kids. Yeah, they ate beans and rice, tacos, but didn't everybody these days? He gave himself a shake and looked back at the crowd.

A roar rose up when Senator Dickenson escorted President Earl onto the stage. Earl didn't start his speech right away. Instead, he walked from side to side, waving, smiling, soaking in the adulation like that desiccated octopus Grant had seen on social media. It had started out as a tiny blob and gradually expanded as people poured water over it until you could finally see what it was. Then it swam away. There was no chance Earl would disappear like that, but he was sure drinking in the love.

The president didn't exactly expand, but he leaned back and basked in the applause and rhythmic chants of the crowd. He pushed his shoulders back, and his normally paper-white skin seemed to flush a light pink as if he were a vampire sucking fresh sustenance from his fans. The chants started with the oldies but goodies from four years ago.

"She's a crook. She's a crook," rang out for what seemed to Grant a full five minutes. It was hard to tell since he was watching for weapons. The chant morphed to "Send them back" for a while, then went on to more recent favorites like "It's a hoax" and "Snyder is a traitor."

Finally, Earl started to speak, but Grant had heard it all so many times it blended in like the radio left on to keep him company on lonely nights. Phrases popped out at him.

". . . the Dems are desperate to prove election fraud, but it's—"

"—a lie," the crowd filled in, glee on their faces.

Grant kept his eyes moving. His eyes caught on a man in a denim jacket and cowboy hat who had a distinct bulge on his belt. He angled around and saw a pouch for a hunting knife hanging empty.

"Aren't my rallies the best?"

The crowd roared their agreement.

"I never had sex with that woman," Earl shouted.

His followers laughed uproariously at this. At least they knew that was a lie, Grant thought.

"I ordered all those people killed?" Earl raised his hands in the air, looking around. "If that's true, why is Murray still around?"

THERESA CRATER

The eruption of applause hurt Grant's ears. Just as it wound down and Earl had taken a breath to shout his next bumper sticker, a block of people in the middle of the auditorium stood up and started shouting, "Time to resign."

The crowd bellowed their disapproval.

The small group brandished signs reading "Lock Him Up" and "Russian Puppet."

Earl crossed his arms and leaned back, shaking his head. He rolled his eyes, a gesture magnified by the video screens around the hall. "Just look at those people over there," he said.

His base shouted louder, almost drowning out the small group. Grant saw a dark-haired man in a black t-shirt and jeans with some kind of an amplifier. He wondered how he'd gotten that through security.

"You know what they deserve," Earl said, his voice booming over the crowd. "Hell, I'll pay your legal fees."

That was all his base needed. Two men climbed over the back of the chairs separating them from the protestors and started swinging. The cops ran for them. Grant and Derrick hung back as they'd been taught to do in situations like this, watching the president to see if anyone separated themselves out and approached him. Or even worse, dropped and aimed. But everyone's attention was on the fracas.

By the time they looked back, about ten men and a few women had joined in the fight. A beefy man in army fatigues tore a sign out of a protestor's hand and started beating him with the stick it was stapled onto. Two cops were dragging one man off another protestor. A line of security pushed and shoved their way around the brawl, trying to separate the two groups and move the protestors toward the door.

Earl leaned forward, his face strawberry red, his lips drawn back in a snarl. "You show 'em."

Senator Dickenson approached him and said something in his ear. Earl shook himself as if coming out of a trance, then shouted, "Okay, Okay. I think that's enough. Let the fine men of the police force do their job and arrest them."

"Lock them up," the crowd chanted. "Lock them up."

Grant didn't think they'd broken any laws. Maybe Earl thought protesting against him was a crime.

After a few more scuffles, the protestors were escorted out and the noise level came down from ear-splitting to a din. Earl raised his hands and the crowd quieted a little more. "Now all you patriots get to the polls. Let's reelect Senator Dickenson here." Earl pounded him on the back and Dickenson winced out a smile. "The lying media says I'm lagging behind Moron Murray."

Loud boos rose up along with shouts of "Bogus news."

Earl leaned back again, his eyes half closed, soaking it in. Then he held a hand up and paused for everyone's attention. "It would be the worst thing if I lost. Very bad. Remember to vote for me!"

The crowd went crazy, taking Grant's full attention. After a while, people filed out of their seats and he confirmed that the president had left the stage. He and Derrick made their way backstage and followed the Ken Dolls to the limos. Grant ended up in Earl's car again. It was his lucky day.

"They love me," Earl said. "Did you see how much they love me?"

"Yes, sir," the Ken Dolls said in unison.

They headed back to the hotel in Atlanta.

# TWELVE

"But we need to go over the debate questions, Mr. President." Earl's top campaign advisor chased him down the hall of the Ritz.

Earl waved him off. "I have the best answers. Besides, my base doesn't care about all that. I know what they want to hear."

"But, sir, your poll numbers are—"

"Fiction. The press makes it all up. Every bit of it."

As Earl continued his charge down the hallway, his campaign advisor threw up his hands. Grant hurried after Earl. The president was safe here, but it was still his job.

Earl turned to him with a leer. "You know what we need." He jerked his head toward the rooms at the other end of the hotel floor they'd been given. Actually, they'd been given three, one on top and one below to ensure security. Three floors just like the three limos.

Grant arrived at the end of the hall and opened the door of the suite. A wave of music and smoke rolled out. Earl stepped in, arms out, waiting for adulation, and the crowd obliged.

"How about a drink?" he shouted.

A waiter handed Earl his favorite Macallan scotch. Brad had been teaching Grant a bit about wine and spirits. This scotch was expensive, and he bet the country was footing the bill.

Donors jockeyed for position to press Earl's hand and talk to him about their various interests. Grant recognized a few of them—representatives of pharmaceuticals, health insurance companies, weapons manufacturers. Daryl Forrest stood at the back of the room, arms crossed in front of his chest. His frown didn't match the sparkle of the diamond-bedecked beauty next to him.

A row of just-budding girls sat on the couch, legs together, hands folded in their laps, faces rapt, awed by the presence of the President of the United States. There was always a group like this everywhere they went. Grant had no idea where they came from. The girls were usually told they'd meet Earl and get a tour of the hotel suite. Maybe get an introduction to a studio head or modeling firm. Grant thought this suite had a kitchen, dining room, sunken entertainment area, grand piano, extensive balcony with bullet-proof panels, and five luxurious bedrooms. Maybe a hot tub at the very back.

A woman with a lot of cleavage and long legs sidled up to Earl and planted a big kiss on his cheek.

"Later, baby." His theatrical whisper reached most ears in the room.

Grant instinctively looked around for Mrs. Earl, even though he knew she was in the matching suite on the south side of the hotel, as far away from all this as she could get. The man she'd been seeing for six years was here for a visit. She'd agreed not to divorce Earl if he won the presidency and been true to her word. But she insisted on seeing Henry at least once a month if not more, even at the height of the campaign.

Grant wasn't sure she'd put up with another four years, but if the polls were right, she wouldn't have to. Plus, they had two convincing body doubles. The real first lady could retire to their private island. Or Earl could buy her a new one. As long as she wasn't seen in public, everything would be fine. Grant used to feel a little sorry for her until Brad had explained she knew exactly what she was getting into when she married Earl.

Speak of the devil. His boss materialized beside him. Maybe there was something to Earl's vampire look and he'd turned Brad one night. That would explain his completely silent approach.

"What?" Grant asked.

"Mr. Forrest is looking a little dour."

Grant tried not to let on he didn't know that word. "Yeah?"

"So what's he all upset about? Did Egorov and Burki read him the riot act?"

"You taught me not to listen."

"For fuck's sake," Brad started.

"You said to watch body language, hands, sudden movements. That listening got people killed."

"It was a secure room. You were supposed to spy on them. Report back."

"You didn't tell me," Grant said between gritted teeth.

Brad shook his head. "Try to remember. What did they talk about?"

Grant squinted his eyes in concentration. The slide of the North Pole swam before his inner eye. "Something about the Arctic. Forrest got really mad."

"About what?"

Grant concentrated. "Something about his company's percentage."

"Did they talk about Earl?"

"They said he had a tiny dick." Grant snorted.

"That is not news. Come on."

"I remember Forrest said they'd asked for an entertainer and that's what he gave them."

"Anything else?"

"They talked about Iran. I guess there's something going on over there." He searched Brad's face for clues.

"Good, anything else?"

Grant shook his head.

Brad patted him on the shoulder. "Good job."

"Oh, after Forrest left, they mentioned something about the Albanian. Do you know who—" Grant stopped dead when he saw Brad's face.

"Are you sure?" Brad asked in a deadly whisper.

"Pretty sure."

Brad looked around the room and motioned for one of the Ken Dolls to come over.

"What is it? Who's the—"

"Shh. Don't say his name."

"Why? Who is he?"

But Brad didn't answer.

The Secret Service agent finally made his way through the crowd. "What's up?"

"I need to talk to Morton," Brad said. "We have intelligence on a possible attempt."

The agent stepped into a quieter spot in the room and pressed his com. "Morton, Red Sky claims to have some intel."

The man listened, then gestured for Brad and Grant to

follow him. He led them halfway down the hall and knocked.

"Come."

He pushed open the door to a bedroom that had been converted into an office. They stepped inside. Grant was surprised by the size. The walls to the several adjacent rooms had been knocked out to form a command center. Morton sat at a desk in the middle. Both sides were dense with equipment.

"Mr. Morton." Brad offered his hand.

Morton suppressed a look of irritation and stretched over the desk to shake it. "Please, have a seat."

Brad sat in one of the chairs in front of the desk and Grant stood behind him.

"I understand you're here to report a threat?"

"Yes, we have reason to believe the Albanian has been hired to assassinate Tycoon."

Grant didn't think Morton seemed surprised.

"You saw him?" Morton asked. "Do you know what he looks like?"

A vein in Brad's neck stood out. Grant knew what this meant and took a step back, but miraculously, Brad sounded civil when he answered.

"No, we heard this in Pristina."

"From whom?" Morton leaned back in his chair, tilting his head at an angle that suggested disbelief.

Brad nodded to Grant.

"Sir, Mr. Rogers here, he asked me to stay behind when the President left the meeting."

Morton raised an eyebrow. "And nobody objected?"

Brad smiled. "Grant has a way of being invisible."

"Go on."

"After their assistant talked about poll numbers, they dismissed him. Then they said they'd call the Albanian."

"I see. What did you think this meant?"

"I didn't know, sir, but Mr. Rogers knows who he is."

Morton steepled his fingers, deep in thought. After a minute, he said, "Thank you for this intel. We'll take it from here."

"Red Sky brought this to you," Brad objected. "We want to be involved."

Morton eyed him, seeming to take his measure. "Be in the conference room across the hall in five minutes."

"We'll be there."

"Just you, Brad."

Brad looked like he would object, but then gave a crisp nod. He stood up and gestured for Grant to follow him. In the hallway, Brad rounded on Grant. "Don't ever call me Mr. Rogers, numb nuts."

"But it's your name."

"Can I help that? It makes me sound like that milk-toast fag who told children they couldn't get flushed down the toilet."

Grant bit his lip to stop himself from smiling. He stood up a bit straighter. "Yes, sir, Brad."

Brad snorted his disgust and stomped off down the hall.

Grant considered himself dismissed and headed to the party room.

# THIRTEEN

Rainey took a circuitous route to the weapons cache. The new location turned out to be an industrial area east of the airport. She passed several abandoned warehouses and small manufacturing shops. She slowed down a few times pretending to search for addresses, making sure she was unobserved. Certain she hadn't been followed, she pulled the Toyota truck into a dirt lot in front of a ramshackle building. A wire metal fence surrounded the property, a bit too new. That would draw an experienced eye, but probably not your average guy tired from a day's work.

Rainey parked and walked across the lot, avoiding a few mud holes. She knocked on a beat-up white metal door and smiled into the security camera. After a minute, the door opened and man who resembled an aged prize fighter stood there, wise eyes over a broad nose, a ragged scar over his left eye.

"As I live and breathe," he said. "My girl Rainey."

"Jim, you're looking good."

He gave her a wry smile and scratched at the gray stubble covering his face. "Not ready for a night out."

"Maybe after the debate," she teased.

He pulled her in for a bear hug that made a few of her vertebrae pop. "Tense?"

"Big job."

"What'cha need?" Jim led her past a series of small offices and opened a door revealing a cavernous space.

Rainey stopped walking, startled to see two HMMWVs parked in front of her. Several jeeps sat partially covered by camouflage tarps. "Wow, expecting some heavy action?"

He chuckled. "Gotta be ready for anything."

"I need a long-range rifle with a silencer and scope."

"Got it. Tripod?"

"Nah, something I can handle on the fly."

Jim eyed her. "How are your range scores lately?"

"Better than last year. I can manage it. But the rifle is back-up. I'm hoping to use a handgun."

"Silencer?"

"Yes, please."

Jim jerked his head toward an alcove. Guns of various sizes covered all three walls. He eyed her and pulled down a Remington CSR. "Try this out."

Rainey checked to see if it was loaded. She found it empty, although she had guessed that by the weight. After loading it, she sighted across the warehouse, practiced picking it up and aiming, timing each attempt. She sat on the bench and took the rifle apart, then reassembled it. Checked her watch again.

"This will do. Do you have a silencer for it?"

Jim handed her one in a canvas zip bag. Rainey took it out and attached it, checked how the rifle handled with it, then returned it to the bag.

Jim watched her, then nodded his approval. "What's your pleasure for a hand-gun?"

"Better give me a Glock. The Secret Service carries a 9mm these days, right?"

"Switched recently."

"That way, if I get discovered, they'll think I'm one of them."

He laughed. "You ain't gonna get discovered."

Rainey paused for a moment to let his confidence in her soak in. She resisted telling him who she was up against. He didn't need to know.

Once she'd secured her weapons and upgraded her binoculars, she gave him a big hug goodbye, then headed back to her hotel room. She picked up some peanut curry on the way. Back in her room, she called Control.

"We think the Albanian drove through one of the small check points on the Canadian border, then took a private jet to Atlanta," he reported. "He didn't go through Harts-field-Jackson. We're checking the municipal airports. If he came in through a private airfield or even the Dobbins Naval Air Reserve, we'll have a harder time identifying the flight."

"You think he came through a military base?"

Control's sigh sounded heavy. "I suppose anything's possible these days. If we could catch him on camera at his start point, we could trace his route."

"Too bad."

"He could be traveling under diplomatic immunity, but I think he's more like you."

"Pardon me?" she objected.

His deep chuckle filled her ear. "He likes to fly under the radar. Do everything on his own."

"I'm talking to you, aren't I?"

"And I'm glad of it." Control's voice was warm. "You're cutting this job close to the wire."

"I'll get it done."

"Once we find the Albanian, we'll let you know."

Rainey finished her curry and leaned back on the bed. She switched on the TV and watched a few minutes of several news channels, gathering in the mood of the country. Early voting put the Murray/Warden ticket ahead, but those were estimates. Coverage of the Springford shooting was dying down, although the news pundits said this should give the advantage to the Democrats and few Republicans who'd spoken up for gun control.

She turned to an international news show for a while. Iceland had lost a second glacier over the summer and put up a plaque to remember the occasion. More saber-rattling from Iran. The country reminded her of a cat cornered by a pack of dogs. She hoped the situation would calm down after she finished her assignment. The stock market had dropped another five percent.

Her cell rang.

"We found his equipment stash. Sending you the address now."

Rainey clicked the link on the screen, then ended the call. A map appeared on her phone. So, he'd holed up close to the coliseum, but not in a hotel. She switched to street view and found an empty lot. Either this picture was out of date or the Albanian had pulled a fast one on Control. She grabbed her pack and Glock, and headed out to the truck. Google estimated the drive at ten minutes, but this was Atlanta and the president was in town. She set the phone to give directions and pulled out.

The GPS kept directing her to streets next to the stadium, but they had been closed off for security. She had to detour every few blocks. She took a roundabout path to Morris Brown College, then made her way through side streets to Beckwith Court. The street curved back around toward the new stadium.

"Your destination is ahead on the right," said the voice of the GPS.

She pulled over just past the big curve and studied the area. What had shown up as an empty lot next to an unnamed street now had a foundation dug out and support beams in place. Looked like they were building a high-end apartment complex. With all the universities and colleges in the area, it could be student housing, but the stadium must be raising real estate prices.

Rainey parked the truck under a tree and stepped onto the sidewalk just south of the construction zone. She crouched behind the bushes, squinting into the growing dark. The whole thing felt fishy, but if she could eliminate him here, it would make her job easier.

She made her silent way across a stubbled field to a large maple and blended with the trunk. Parked on the edge of the site was a big yellow excavator and backhoe. She slipped between them and crouched behind the front of the tread, studying the place. The sun lowered toward the horizon and long shadows fell across the red dirt. The trailer hosting the office for the build sat on one corner of the big lot, its windows dark.

She doubted the Albanian had stashed anything on this site. It looked too active. They'd probably closed it down for the debates. The Secret Service tended to create a dead zone around a presidential event for a few days before, sending everyone off on unexpected holidays. The workers loved it, but they got a lot of complaints from company owners.

Or this was a set up. He must have spotted her in the

coliseum and arranged to be seen here. It was the perfect place for an ambush. She'd have to be careful.

Rainey pulled out her Glock. The silencer was already on. She slammed in the magazine and charged a round into the chamber. Drawing on her training at the nunnery, she settled her breath and let her awareness flood out into her surroundings. The hum of traffic formed a background. A robin called from a nearby tree. No shuffle of footsteps. No rustling from underbrush disturbed the place. The faint scent of fresh baked bread wafted from behind her.

She scanned for hiding places. The cement truck parked next to the backhoe. The tarp covering a pile of lumber across the way. She squinted to see if the floor had been poured. He could be in the hole. Behind the stack of support beams. In the trailer. Behind it. Between the row of shipping containers on the other side of the site. Rainey didn't know the Albanian well enough to guess his strategy.

The sun set and the shadows deepened. Streetlights switched on. A faint breeze blew a thin line of silt down from the bucket of the machine she crouched beside. At that moment, the cicadas sent up a shrill in unison. The insects almost drowned out sound. Was someone above her?

Rainey rolled. Came up to her feet, gun aimed high.

A heavy weight fell on her, knocking her to the ground. Her attacker let out a grunt, reached around, trying to trap her arms.

The Albanian.

Rainey thrashed back and forth, pushing against solid muscle, trying to make room for a punch.

"*Cyka*," Dushku muttered.

Rainey recognized the word. *Bitch*. It sent another surge

of adrenaline through her. She grappled with his arms, pushing against him, trying to bring her legs up.

"Oh, you want?" Dushku asked.

Pure rage took her. She howled, got her knees under his hips, and pushed.

Dushku flew back.

Rainey rolled, stretched out her arms, searching the ground for her gun.

Nothing.

She jumped to her feet and took a fighting stance.

The light from the street fell on his scared face. Brown hair spiked on top. Gray, grizzled whiskers. A scar ran from the edge of one eye and disappeared behind his ear. Muscled, light on his feet.

Almost a handsome pirate, Rainey thought.

"Oh, you want to play first."

A wave of disgust rolled through her, but Rainey shook it off. No time for that.

Dushku circled, then struck, fast as a mamba. Rainey bobbed to the right, moved around him, and cuffed him hard on the ear as he passed.

He swirled around. A roundhouse punch headed for her temple.

She ducked and landed a hard blow to his kidney. She was rewarded with a grunt. She stood and danced back, but he wasn't in front of her anymore.

Just as she turned, arms like steel bands grabbed her. She stomped on his foot, but he just laughed.

He pulled her against him.

She stiffened her fingers and pushed back, reaching for his eyes.

He grabbed her throat and squeezed.

She scrunched up her neck and searched for his little finger, the weakest link, but he had something thick wrapped around his hands and she couldn't reach them. Dark spots floated in the air in front of her.

She pushed up and slammed the back of her head against his nose.

"*Dermo,*" he hissed. Shit.

His grip loosened and she surged forward, breaking his hold.

She searched wildly for a weapon. A steel bar leaned against the backhoe. She ran toward it, but he tripped her. She fell hard.

Dushku landed on her like a wrestler jumping from the ropes. The impact drove the breath from her lungs. She struggled for air, but he grabbed her around the neck and squeezed again.

Rainey went still, but Dushku kept squeezing. She let herself go limp. Her vision started to dim. She steeled herself not to move.

Dushku gave a satisfied grunt and flipped her over.

Rainey punched him in the throat and he gagged. She jumped up and pummeled him. He fell under her rain of blows. She stomped on his head.

Police sirens sounded just next to the site. "Hands up. Don't move." The voice was close.

Rainey scuttled back into the shadows.

The glint of metal caught her attention. Her gun.

She picked it up, stepped behind a large container, and got off a shot at the Albanian.

Too fast. The bullet pinged off the metal of the cement truck.

A bullet puffed up sand right next to her.

"Drop the weapon."

Could the police see her? She couldn't get caught. Not now.

Rainey turned on her heel and ran, her Nike Vaporflies silent on the hardpack.

She quietly blessed Arnold.

She hid behind a hydrangea bush on the edge of the sidewalk. A patrol car sat next to her white truck, two officers standing near it, guns drawn.

More gun fire came from behind her.

Next a shout loud enough for her to make out. "Officer down. Officer down."

The two policemen listened to their coms, then ran into the bushes separating the street from the construction site.

Rainey waited. Detached the silencer and stowed it in her pocket. Stuffed the gun in the waist band of her pants and made her noiseless way through the bushes. Nobody on the street.

In one short sprint, she jumped into the white Toyota truck and turned around, careful not to let her tires squeal. Heading up Walnut toward M.L.K. Jr. Dr., two ambulances and a bevy of police cars passed her, sirens wailing.

Looked like Dushku had shot his way out. Unless one of those ambulances was for him. She didn't know.

But one thing was certain. He had seen her face.

She headed for the airport and drove into the long-term parking lot, scanning for cameras. She found a spot where she was shielded by a large van and parked. The cops had the license plate and if one of them had been killed, they'd be hot on her trail. She stuck on her Shiva baseball cap and walked around until she found an SUV that would do. It only took a minute to unlock the door and hotwire it. She hoped the owners were on a long vacation.

She should have known it had been a set up as soon as she saw the construction site. She shook her head.

*That was sloppy, Rain.*

# FOURTEEN

News of the presidential debates filled Atlanta's early morning news, but at last Rainey was rewarded by a report on the police shooting.

"Last night, Officer Jayden Smith was gunned down when police were called to the scene of a fight at a construction site just south of the Mercedes-Benz Stadium. Presidential debates are scheduled there for this evening, and police feared a security breach. Officer Smith was shot execution style, two shots to the chest and one to the head, leading police to believe gang violence."

Rainey shook her head.

The coverage switched to a picture of a couple in their late twenties perhaps, the woman holding a baby outside a nice home.

"Officer Smith leaves behind a wife and eight-month-old daughter. The suspect is still at large."

Rainey shook her head. Another child without a father. Maybe she could send an anonymous donation. She muted the sound. So the Albanian had survived. Just as she'd suspected. It would have been too much to hope the police had put him out of action. No such luck. The job was still hers.

BRAD ASSEMBLED the team early on the morning of the debate. Grant's vision was still a bit blurred and his stomach threatened to empty its contents on the conference room table. What the fuck time was it, anyway?

His eyes strayed to the wall. Seven o'clock in the morning.

"We've got a real job, now," Brad said, his voice eager.

Grant remembered watching the sun rise before he'd fallen into the bed and finally slept. He rubbed his gritty eyes.

Last night, he'd followed Earl into the party room and gotten swept into a fantasy world. Stunning women. Rich, powerful men. He remembered Earl handing him a glass of his pricey Scotch, pounding him on the back, and saying, "Go have fun. We're safe in here."

Grant lost track of how much he drank. The expensive stuff disappeared with Earl into a back bedroom where he heard some screaming behind a closed door. He'd spent the night with the new love of his life. Betty—petite, brunette, with a cute giggle. Said she was a model.

Grant closed his eyes, savoring it all again.

"Did you all hear me?" Brad slammed his fist down on the table.

Grant jerked upright.

"We have a credible threat. Morton thinks it might be a high-level assassin targeting Earl. We need to run a tight ship today."

"Do we have a description of this guy?" George asked.

"No, but you should look for anything big enough to hold a weapon. Check all the closets, small rooms. Watch the concession deliveries."

"That's a big place for the three of us."

"The other agencies are searching, too. We've got the right side of the stadium floor which we'll split with two of the Ken Dolls. Also, the top two tiers. Cobra Squad will follow us an hour later."

"Yes, sir."

He eyed Grant. "We can party when we get to the Keys. Derrick, George, you take Grant here and sober him up. Then get over to the coliseum. I'll meet you there in an hour."

Derrick pulled Grant from his chair and marched him down the hall and into their suite. He turned on the shower and shoved Grant into it fully clothed.

The needles of cold water penetrated the fog.

"Jesus Christ, man. What the—" Water squirted up his nose and he sputtered.

"George, would you mind getting us an espresso from the mess hall?"

"Sure thing."

Grant heard a door slam.

Derrick leaned against the shower stall, one hand on each side, blocking him in. "Feeling better yet?"

"I'm fucking freezing, man. Let me out of here."

Derrick reached around and turned off the water. "Strip off those clothes and then take a real shower. How's your stomach?"

"A little better."

"Good. Do you want to eat?"

A wave of nausea hit him. "Naw. Not yet."

Grant dressed and sipped the espresso until his head cleared a bit, then the three of them headed out.

The noise level at the Mercedes-Benz Stadium made Grant grind his teeth. He stopped off at a booth to buy some aspirin and a soda. The woman stared at him, so he tried to remember what they called it in the South. "Pop. Give me a pop."

"Yes, sir."

He tore open the foil aspirin container and swallowed four.

"All right?" Derrick asked.

"Yeah."

"How should we do this?" George asked.

"Let's split up. I'll take the floor here and meet up with Brad when he shows up. Grant, you take hallways leading to the ceiling access. George, you're on the floor below."

"Roger that," they said in unison.

They checked their coms, then headed off.

The place was crawling with security teams. Grant pushed the elevator button for the top floor and stepped out into relative quiet. He breathed a sigh of relief. Leaned against the wall for a few minutes just to catch up with himself, then pushed off and started his inspection.

Routine. With the master key, he opened every door to every closet, cubbyhole, bathroom, and utility room, giving each a cursory sweep. The whole search took just over four hours.

His stomach started to grumble, so he called in an all clear and headed down to the food courts. He passed another security guy with spikey brown hair. He wore a black uniform with a Cobra Squad insignia on the sleeve and sported quite a scar on his face. They nodded, professional to professional, and Grant headed down to get lunch.

# FIFTEEN

The Albanian shifted the canvas bag to his left shoulder and nodded at the Red Sky agent walking by. The more private security the better, as far as he was concerned. The multinationals all did business with him and were more than willing to hand over their uniforms for his missions. At this point, he and his men could pass as a member of any of them.

After escaping from the police last night, he'd sketched the other assassin's face from memory. Granted, he hadn't gotten a leisurely look at her, but he did his best. He took a picture of the drawing with his phone, then uploaded it to the SVR servers.

Nothing.

That probably meant his sketch hadn't been accurate enough. Then he scanned for female agents, African American, Indian, Asian—hell, it had been impossible to determine in the dark. He didn't find anyone resembling her. He'd sent the sketch to Kiselev's assistant in case he could find a lead.

He continued down the hallway, grateful he didn't pass

anyone else. He'd already moved his equipment to the service room he'd picked as a second choice, but after last night's encounter, he changed his mind. He would set up behind the mechanism that ran the retractable roof. More secure. The shot would be harder, but he could manage it.

He continued around the slow curve of the coliseum. Near the room holding the roof machinery, he spotted a handy closet across the hall. He picked the lock and dumped his gear except for his scope, then crossed the hallway and broke into the ceiling control room.

"Hey, nobody's allowed in here," came a shout. A man in a blue hard hat walked toward him.

"Just doing a security sweep."

"They already did one earlier."

"Yeah, they've doubled up. Maybe tripled. Apparently, there's some kind of threat."

The worker looked at the lanyard ID that Dushku had stolen last night and doctored to add his own photo. "Should we wish him luck?" he whispered, a mischievous look on his face.

Dushku chuckled. "Know what you mean. So, I'm supposed to slap a seal on the door. How long you going to be?"

It was too early to take the guy out. He'd be missed this afternoon.

"Just finishing up."

"Should I check back in fifteen?"

"Sounds good."

Dushku turned to leave.

"Hey, you know I was joking, right?"

Dushku tried for a good guy smile. "Sure. No problem."

He headed around the curve of the hall, then decided to go down and get his food and water provisions topped off.

Once he camped out in the ceiling control room, he would stay until the job was done.

At one of the concessions downstairs, he bought a pastrami on rye, then went to another store and picked up a packaged roast beef sandwich and large water. Further down, he bought another packaged sandwich, tuna on white, and two bottles of water.

He headed back up. On his way toward the room, he slapped a couple of seals on doors that led to the lights and scrawled indecipherable initials on them. He knew Cobra Squad would be using these seals after they finished their last sweep.

He was happy to find the control room empty this time. He made his way out onto the platform that led to the fixed trichord truss and studied the roof. The system was enormous. An impressive piece of engineering.

He walked down the truss a few feet and the stage came into view. There was enough room for the tripod. He took out his scope and studied the line of sight. A longer distance. He'd have to be precise to shoot between two steel beams that held a truss in place, but he could do it.

With a satisfied grunt, he retrieved his gear and put a seal on the door before he closed it, hoping it would cover the crack. Then he sat on the floor and ate his pastrami while it was still warm. He unpacked and checked his gun. He'd cleaned it last night, but he took it apart and cleaned it again. Checked the scope, the silencer. He couldn't risk setting up yet. Too much time to be discovered. He'd wait until the crowd was here making a big ruckus. Right before the candidates were introduced.

After he finished preparing his kit, he settled down for a nap. Best be sharp for the night's work.

# SIXTEEN

Rainey blended with the long lines still waiting to get into the Mercedes-Benz Stadium. Morton had slipped her a security pass earlier in the day, and she'd stashed her guns inside and spent time studying the catwalks to the large spotlights. The Albanian was nowhere to be seen. He'd cleared out the utility room where she found his tripod. He'd picked a new spot. But where?

The crowd was a sea of t-shirts decorated with candidates' faces or campaign slogans. Many people sported the ubiquitous campaign baseball cap from four years ago. They'd have to take them off to pass through security.

Shirts and buttons with slogans about various social problems dotted the crowd. She was happy to see a number about the environment. Some insulted the other candidate. "Reelect Egorov" was her favorite. One guy's had a picture of Earl on a leash, both he and the Russian president in leathers. She doubted he'd get through the night unscathed.

Sporadic political chants broke out from time to time. The atmosphere crackled with excitement. Young men and women made their way through the crowds seeking signatures for various petitions. Two men in front of her exchanged insults with each other, but they seemed almost jovial. No fights so far. People wanted to get inside and not be carted off before the big show. Rainey hoped there was a ruckus. It would make a perfect distraction for her kill shot if it came at the right moment.

The line got closer to the first set of metal detectors. She darted to the right and approached a side door, presented her pass, and made her way through the throngs inside, giving her apologies to several idealists asking for donations for their causes. Rainey ran up the stairs to the top floor, waking up her legs and getting her blood pumping. She needed to be alert and ready for action.

Upstairs was closed to the public. The hallway stretched, silent. She passed a pair of Cobra Squad guards, flashed her badge, and kept walking. When she reached the door to the utility room she'd chosen, luck was with her. The hall was empty. She quickly picked the lock, pulled the security seal off the crack, and slipped inside, hoping the seal would flap back in place.

Earlier, Rainey had left the door to the catwalk unlocked. She crept out. Put her scope to her eye and scanned all the beams holding the spotlights. No sign of the Albanian. She sat against the wall and watched people far below. Local candidates had already started speaking, but nobody paid them any mind except the Atlanta news media.

Sitting in the shadow, the seething mass of people below her, she reviewed her situation. If this was her assignment and her initial plan had been discovered, what would she do? Probably pick a different place, not another spotlight. Rainey walked to the end of the catwalk and stepped over onto the beam. She flattened out and inch-wormed her way to the lights. Leaning against the housing of the spots, she methodically studied her surroundings.

Rainey felt certain the Albanian would pick a high spot to shoot from. He wouldn't have had the time to change up his weapons. At least she didn't think so. The trusses holding the roof in place might serve. She studied each one, but saw nothing out of the ordinary. No people this high up. Access to the roof had been shut down even to security teams.

Then again, maybe the Albanian would depend on her thinking he'd change his plans. Maybe he was waiting behind one of the utility room doors, preparing to sneak out to the lights, set up quickly, and shoot. She'd just have to be ready for him to appear from any direction. But she wanted to catch him in a room and not on the precarious catwalks where he might fall into the audience below and make a huge splash, so to speak.

A huge roar went up from the crowd below. The TBS anchors' faces flashed huge on the video screens. They appeared to be announcing the rules of the debate. Or trying to. The crowd broke into rival chants—"Four more years" vs. "I'm all in," which was the vice president's slogan, but it was catchy.

The crowd noise went up several decibels when President Earl walked out, clapping for himself, pointing at people in the audience, a huge smile plastered on his face. The make-up people had given him a touch of color on his cheeks so he wouldn't resemble Count Dracula quite so much in his funereal black suit.

Senator Murray came out next and was greeted by a roar. If decibels decided the election, he would win hands down. The two shook hands and took their places behind their respective mikes. The TBS anchors pleaded with the crowd to quiet down. It took about three minutes.

". . . taking time from your candidates," was finally heard as the crowd settled.

Opening statements began.

Rainey kept her attention on her job, scanning the roof, spotlights, trusses, and catwalks. Just as Murray was wrapping up his introduction, a door opened.

A figure in black snuck out, a gray duffle bag slung over one shoulder.

So, he'd picked the housing for retracting the roof. A difficult shot. She had to hand it to him.

While he climbed, Rainey balanced on the thin beam and made her way back to the utility room as fast as she dared. Once on firm ground, she pulled up the blueprints of the building as she moved into the hallway.

Left.

She set off at a dead run. When the door to the ceiling control room was in sight, she paused in an alcove. Pulled her gun and attached the silencer, then tiptoed to the entrance.

The seal still covered the crack between the door and the frame. How had he managed that?

She knelt down and picked the lock as silently as possible. Pushed the door open slowly. It swung open fully just as the Albanian came back into the room to fetch the rest of his gear.

Rainey aimed.

The Albanian jumped back through the door and disappeared. The shot pinged off a truss outside. Would any security forces hear it?

Rainey covered the room in two steps. Stopped and listened.

Nothing but the sound of Earl's nasal voice and the subdued mumble of the crowd rose from below.

The Albanian couldn't take his shot yet. He was still assembling his gear. Rainey picked up the second duffle bag and threw it outside in the hall. Slammed the door. Then she moved toward the door that opened to the stadium roof, every nerve taut.

She stepped out onto the webbing of the catwalk, pointed her weapon left, then whirled to the right. Looked up.

The space was empty.

She crept toward the ladder that led to the top of the box holding the retracting machinery, her gun trained upward.

A sudden blow from behind knocked her forward. She almost lost her footing, but regained it and swirled right into a punch to the gut.

Rainey fell and the Albanian went down with her, knocking her gun away. He kicked her toward the edge of the walkway. Her head and shoulders went over.

He pushed again.

Rainey hung in mid-air, one leg hooked over a bar supporting the handrail. She let herself drop, then used the momentum to swing around and grab the railing farther away from her assailant. She released her leg's hold on the bar and used the motion to swing again, this time landing more fully on the catwalk.

The Albanian rushed her. She surged up, banging the top of her head under his chin. He fell back. She followed, raining down blows, kicking him.

He rolled and came to his feet.

Rainey spotted her weapon, dipped down to grab it.

The Albanian kicked her in the ribs. He was a black

shadow outlined in light. Rainey realized he was standing in the control room door. She rushed him, pushing him through.

He fell.

Rainey aimed and fired three shots. Two to the chest. One to the head.

The door to the hallway burst open.

A Red Sky agent ran into the room, gun drawn.

"Don't move," he shouted.

Rainey put her hands up.

"Drop the gun."

She slowly lowered her weapon to the floor and kicked it to the side.

She stood back up and recognized the man holding a gun on her. Grant Mendez. A member of her squadron in Afghanistan. One of the men who'd attacked her.

She shook her head against a flood of images. Four men grabbing her. Driving her out to a secluded spot in the desert. Staking her out on the ground.

Grant checked the Albanian's pulse. An invitation to escape, but Rainey stayed her ground, still in the grip of memories.

The flash of a knife cutting her clothes off. They left her underwear for Brad to rip off. Then he plunged into her.

She winced and forced herself back to the present moment. Grant was staring at the body on the ground.

"The assassin," she said.

"You got him." Grant was still staring at the dead body on the floor, watching the blood pool behind his head. "We heard someone was after Earl."

The pounding inside her. Over and over. One man after another. Slapping and punching. Calling her names.

She shook her head again to focus.

"You'll find his rifle in that bag in the hall. He already took the tripod up to the top of the box outside. Now, if you'll excuse me."

Grant looked up. "Great. Thank you."

Then his eyes went wide. "Madison?"

Her old name. The name of the woman who died. She remembered the relief as she flew out of her battered body while a man rutted on top of her, his hands wrapped around her neck, squeezing.

The light healing all that it touched as she swam up into it. The all-encompassing love.

"But you're supposed to be dead."

"I was," Rainey said, studying Grant carefully. "They sent me back to do some clean up."

Beings of light had handed her the list in that threshold before the tunnel of light that she wanted to fly through with every fiber of her consciousness. She'd known what they were asking without any words being exchanged. As soon as her glowing fingers closed around the scroll held out to her, she returned with a whoosh and woke in a local hospital with ER workers shouting over her body.

She'd been reborn as Rainey.

"They?" Grant blew out a breath like he'd been punched in the gut. "But I checked. You had no pulse."

"That's right."

Grant stared at her, his mouth working. Then his face crumpled. "I tried. I swear I tried to stop them."

"No you didn't," Rainey said, calm now.

"They would have killed me."

"Better me than you?"

His body collapsed into itself. "I'm sorry. I thought they'd stop, that they'd run out of steam." He shook his head, eyes closed against the memory. "But they came back again. Every one of them. Brad told me it was my turn, but you were such a bloody mess. I checked for a pulse and told them you were gone. They told me it didn't matter, but I said I wasn't boning no fucking corpse."

He flinched, realizing what he'd said. "I thought you were dead," he whispered again. "Out of your misery. I'm . . ." He opened his palms out, then shook his head. Tears ran down his face.

"Where's Brad?" Rainey asked in an even voice.

"You going to kill him, too?"

Rainey made a small sound of irritation. "No, where is he?"

"Behind the stage. Guarding the doors to the back."

"Give me five minutes, then call him on your com."

"What?" Grant looked lost.

"Tell him you found the Albanian. That you killed him."

Grant seemed to have forgotten about the body on the floor of the utility room. "But you did."

"Right, but remember? I'm dead."

Grant's mouth worked.

Rainey put her hands on his shoulders and shook him gently. "Look at me. Tell him you heard a sound and came in to check. That you found this man with a gun." She pointed to her own gun on the floor.

Grant was nodding his head now.

"That you fought and took it away from him, turned it on him and shot him."

Grant frowned. "He'll never believe that. He thinks I'm . . ."

"Lame?" Rainey offered.

Grant snorted. "Yeah."

"He'll never think that again. That's my gift to you."

"But, why would you?"

"Because I want them all to think I'm dead. Can you do that? Can you keep my secret?"

A look of gratitude flooded Grant's face, then his eyes teared up. "I'm so sorry."

Rainey wiped her gun down, removing all trace of her fingerprints, and handed it to Grant. "Five minutes."

"I'll never be able to repay you."

Rainey gave him a wry smile. "Don't worry. I'm sure the universe will figure something out."

"Huh?"

"Never mind. Now repeat your story."

Grant stumbled through it, but hit all the key points.

She thumped him on the shoulder. "Good. Now, I'm going. Give me five minutes."

# SEVENTEEN

K iselev gave a grunt of surprise when he saw the number on his phone. He answered it with a curt, "Report?"

"He's dead, sir."

Kiselev glanced up at the flat screen TV playing on mute. "Why hasn't it hit the news yet?"

"Not the target. The man you sent."

"What?" Kiselev paused in disbelief. "Who did it?"

"Man from Red Sky claims he heard a noise and surprised him."

"Do you believe him?"

"It seems unlikely, sir. He's a bit of a dufus."

He frowned. "Dufus? What does that mean?"

"Not very smart. Doubtful he could get the drop on somebody like Dushku."

"What's your theory?"

"One of my men saw a woman leaving with a big duffle bag. Exactly what I'd use to hide a sniper rifle."

"A woman." Kiselev's lip curled in disgust.

"Yes, sir."

"Was he killed by a sniper?"

"No, a handgun. Glock 9mm. What we carry."

"What is Red Sky's standard issue?"

"They prefer Berettas. But the man claims he took the gun away from Dushku."

Kiselev snorted. "He's not the killer then."

"Agreed."

Kiselev thought of the sketch he'd gotten from Dushku. "Did you get a picture of this woman with the duffle bag?"

"I haven't had time to search the data base."

"Did you get a look at her?"

"No, but my guy described her."

"And?"

"Five-seven. Light skinned African American. Maybe Indian or South Asian. A bit of black hair under her base-ball cap. Curly, but not like an Afro. We couldn't see her face."

"Thank you." Kiselev ended the call.

Kiselev texted the man he'd sent to kill this female assassin. "Report back to home base immediately." The man knew what this meant. Kiselev hoped he didn't run. It would just make more work. There was no place he could hide from Kiselev's network, though.

The Russian oligarch sat deep in thought, swirling the bourbon in his glass, but not drinking. He stared out at the green meadows of his compound. What was the little minx up to? If she wanted to rub out Earl, she'd have just let Dushku finish the job. Maybe she was one of Morton's hires. Intelligence suggested he sometimes had a freelance agent test his security. That must be it. But where would she be now?

He lifted the bourbon to his lips, but the ice had melted. He set the glass down. Morton probably wasn't done with her. She'd stick with Earl. He'd have to send in someone to take them both out.

He sent a copy of Dushku's sketch of the woman to another agent he had stationed near Earl's private retreat. "The Albanian down. This is the suspect. Sketch not precise. Locate and terminate." He attached a picture of Earl. "This is your second target."

"*Zametano*," came the text back, the Russian equivalent of "Roger that."

Kiselev had hoped for a big, splashy kill. He'd have to settle for something a little quieter, but it would still get the job done.

# EIGHTEEN

Rainey sprinted down the hall of the top floor of the Mercedes-Benz Stadium, picked up the sniper rifle and ammo she'd stashed earlier in the day, then took the stairs down two at a time. Before pushing out onto the main floor, she put on the baseball cap and lowered it over her face. She pushed the door open and slowed down, stopping from time to time to look at the displays in the booths. Across from her, two Secret Service agents put their hands to their coms, listening intently. Then they jogged to the stairs and disappeared.

Word was out.

Rainey made her way through the choked lobby, smiling at all the people asking for her signature, shaking her head no to all the people shoving leaflets in her face, and finally reached the front door. She flashed her Secret Service security badge at a policeman and walked around the containment area with the metal detectors. Rounded the tented area and hurried to her SUV. She'd pack up her hotel room, drop the guns off with Jim, and fly to Miami.

∼

Jim sat sprawled in his office chair watching the debate, which was just now winding up. He sat up with a look of surprise. "Job done?"

"All finished. Nothing on the news?"

"Just that buffoon yelling and the other guy trying to be sensible. In my humble opinion."

"Good." Rainey dropped the bag. "I lost one gun."

Jim shrugged. "It happens."

"I assume they're untraceable."

"You assume right." He picked up the pot from an old battered coffee maker and whirled the dark liquid around. "Cup?"

"Wish I could. Gotta run."

"You ain't done yet?"

Rainey smiled at him. "No, now for the main event. Do you have a syringe?"

Jim looked confused. "Uh, yeah."

"Thanks."

He handed her a syringe in a plastic container. "Real deadly weapon," he quipped.

"Let's hope so." She stuffed it into her bag.

"Best of luck. Next time you're in town, let's go to that new Caribbean vegan place. You might like it."

"They've got a restaurant like that?"

"Sure do. This is Atlanta." He winked.

She gave him a snappy salute and turned on her heel. She headed for the airport. Once in the long-term lot, she wiped the SUV for fingerprints, picked up a hundred-dollar bill with a tissue and left it on the driver's seat to pay for repairs to the dash where she'd hot-wired the car. She headed into the terminal.

Flights to Miami left almost every hour. Rainey picked a different airline from the one she'd flown in on, using the identity Control had cooked up for this hit, and took the train to her terminal. Walking along with the crowd, she kept an eye out for anyone following her. Looked like she was in the clear.

Then someone bumped into her. Apologized. She turned, but he'd already ducked into the crowd. Maybe running for his flight. Maybe not.

On the plane, she settled in until they reached cruising altitude. She took off her jacket and searched the back and sleeves. Under the collar, she found a tiny tracking device. She tore out a small corner from the onboard magazine, then lifted off the tracker, pressed it onto the piece of paper, and palmed it.

Soon, the beverage cart lumbered down the aisle. The flight attendant stretched over Rainey to give the man in the window seat his beer, and she slipped the tracker into the woman's pocket.

"What can I get you, ma'am?"

"Nothing for me, thanks."

The cart moved on.

Now she had to figure out who was following her as well as how to get to Earl's island and complete her mission.

"You killed the Albanian? You expect us to believe that?" Brad shook his head.

"Believe what you like." Grant sat back in the chair, attempting nonchalance, but sweat beaded his forehead.

They were sitting in Morton's office back at the hotel.

Morton let the Red Sky captain interrogate his man, although he guessed who had really killed Dushku. His girl Rainey. Thank heaven. He just couldn't figure how she'd done it.

Red Sky had sent in their cleaners to remove all the blood from the floor. Morton personally confirmed the identity of the Albanian, then the cleaners took the body out stuffed in a large cart. After the debate, Morton's team secured the candidates, which meant Earl was now in the hotel roaming the hallway looking for another party. Nobody had told him about the assassination attempt. He'd probably tweet about it.

"Tell us again," Brad said.

Grant repeated his story for the umpteenth time. "I was on a routine sweep, heard a noise, opened the door. Took the guy by surprise. Tackled him and took his gun. Shot him."

Brad just stared at him, shaking his head.

"Who was this guy, anyway?" Grant asked.

"He was infamous. Used to be head of intelligence in Albania. He tortured people—skinned them alive, dunked them in boiling water, but didn't let them die. Put them in those medieval cages and stuck lances through them. Didn't let them die. After the regime he worked for lost power, he ran an international group of assassins for hire. How could you have gotten the drop on him?"

Grant turned a little green. "I've been working out. Training extra."

"Bullshit."

Brad took a breath to ask more questions, but Morton waved his hand. "That's enough. The Albanian is dead, and we owe your agency a debt."

This stopped Brad. He glared at Grant as if to say this

wasn't over, then nodded. "Thank you, sir. I'm glad we got the bastard."

"Let's double security until after the election," Morton said. "Liaise with Stan."

"Yes, sir." Brad saluted, then seemed to remember he wasn't in the army anymore.

"That will be all."

The two men left the room and Morton looked around. Two agents were huddled together across the long room. Nobody was close to him. He took out one of his burner phones and sent a text to the one number on it. "Thanks. Owe you one."

After a minute, a smiley face appeared on his screen.

CHAPTER

# NINETEEN

Boris Ivanov stared at his phone, watching the red dot sitting at the Atlanta airport. Take-off had been delayed. Current estimates were that she'd land in another two hours so he had some time to research who this woman was.

He'd wormed his way into the U.S. government databases and activated a face recognition program that compared the sketch from Kiselev with employee photos past and present. Just under two thousand possible hits came back. Now he added some limiting terms, starting with military service, and did a second search.

He hit return. "Go get her."

While he waited, Boris looked through the take-out menus in the hotel information notebook and decided to try Cuban. Miami or Havana were the best places for it. He ordered the short rib boliche and tres leches to go.

"Your dinner will be ready in twenty minutes, Mr. Smith."

He always used the name Smith. Impossible to trace. "Thank you."

Best to fill up now. It might be a long night.

He grabbed his keys and went for the food. By the time he got back, his computer displayed twenty candidates. He ate at the round table in the room and clicked through the options.

The first three women were Caucasian. Their fancy curls courtesy of a beauty salon had triggered the program. Two candidates met the racial possibilities, but both were on active duty in combat zones. The next woman looked very much like the sketch he'd gotten from Kiselev. He clicked on the woman's military service records and skimmed through them.

*Madison Danika Kumara.*

*Joined the Marines just out of high school and served in Afghanistan. Died from wounds sustained in a "combat related incident" in Tarin Kowt, Uruzgan Province in 2014 during second tour of duty.*

Bingo. This was his girl. Died.

Right.

She was special ops, for sure. Officially dead, but as alive as he was. But was she CIA or private security? Something else?

He logged into the SVR's servers and did a search using her name. Russia's Foreign Intelligence Service would have her on file no matter how deep her cover was.

He finished his meal while he waited. Wiping his hands on a napkin, he picked up his phone and brought up Earl's schedule. The president would be in Miami tomorrow morning, then head straight to Ibis Island. He reviewed Earl's house in the Keys and the surrounding land.

He texted Kiselev and asked for an invitation to be forwarded for him to attend Earl's Halloween celebration.

That would get him on site most easily. He started studying the blueprints.

After five minutes, the computer dinged again. That had taken a long time. He nudged the mouse and the screen sprang to life.

*No Search Results*

That was impossible. He copied the picture from her military records and loaded it to the SVR servers. Grabbed another beer out of the fridge. He sat back on the bed. The headboard bounced against the wall. Nothing ever worked right in these cheap-ass places, but here he could be anonymous. Pass for Mr. America on a trip to beautiful Miami.

What was taking so long? He moved over to the round table where his computer sat and nudged it again. He was rewarded with a little spinning ball with the SVR logo at the top of the screen. He checked the clock. Five minutes had gone by. He smoked another cigarette, ignoring the no smoking sign, and finally the computer dinged.

*Born in Brooklyn in 1995 to Imani* née *Russell and Bhupen Varma.*

*Mother African American from South Carolina. Legal assistant.*

*Father Indian, born in Bombay, immigrated in 1985. Worked in tech until the bubble burst. Later worked as clerk for the airlines.*

*Subject joined Marines just out of high school to help family financially.*

*Deceased.*

"Well, I'll be damned," he said. She had eluded the SVR. Somebody must have scrubbed her record. Somebody very talented.

An alarm sounded indicating the flight to Miami was twenty minutes out. Boris checked the little red dot on the map. The plane was stacked up, waiting for its turn to land. It would be delayed, but it was time to go.

Traffic was heavy on the freeway and what Google Maps said would take ten minutes ended up taking half an hour. He kept checking his tracker. She was at the gate. Must be a big plane and unloading slowly.

Boris pulled into short term parking and made his way into the main terminal. He bought a cup of coffee and settled in front of Starbucks close to where returning passengers spilled out from Concourse D. He checked the tracker again.

Her plane had landed twenty minutes ago. Boris enlarged the screen and the Miami airport structure swam into view. The red dot blinked close to D22. Hell, she hadn't left the gate yet. Was she meeting a contact? He'd give her another fifteen minutes.

He still couldn't believe the Albanian was gone. The man had been a legend—ruthless, shrewd, relentless, and the best fighter he knew. She must have taken him by surprise. Seduced him and struck when he was distracted. Although he'd known Dushku to fuck women with a gun to their head more often than not. He'd find the bitch and kill her. Get revenge for one of the greats.

Boris checked the red dot again and snorted. The tracker indicated she was in the air flying north.

"*Yebat*," he shouted. Then looked around quickly. A few people had started at his loud voice, but nobody recognized the Russian word for 'fuck'.

He called his asset in Atlanta. "Check your screen," he said.

"What?"

"Just check it."

"What the— She's coming back?

"I doubt that. She found your tracker and left it on the plane more likely. But when the plane lands, be there."

"Yes, sir."

Jumping to his feet, Boris walked toward the security office. He had to force himself not to run. That would draw attention. When he was close, he found a vantage point behind a newspaper dispenser. It looked like there was one guy watching the cameras at the moment. His luck was holding.

He crept up to the office and shone a black light onto the keypad outside the door. He found the numbers with the most fingerprints. Pushing them at random, he wondered how many mistakes he'd be allowed before the thing shut down. The third try rewarded him with a green light and a beep.

He walked in, waved, and smiled. He flashed a generic fake badge he kept for such occasions. "U.S. Marshall."

The security worker was young, late teens, maybe in his early twenties. Still graced with the pimples of adolescence. His crew cut spoke of an attempt at toughness.

"I need to look for somebody. Can you help me?"

"Yeess," the man stuttered.

"Good boy. Now, show me D22 from an hour and a half ago." He slapped a photo of Madison he'd pulled from her records on the desk. "This is who we're looking for."

"Why do you—"

"Escaped murderer, I'm afraid," Boris said. That was close to the truth. He pointed at the monitor. "I need you to keep your eyes peeled."

The man nodded and pushed a few buttons. The gate was empty.

"Can you speed it up?"

The image jumped a bit, but the gate remained empty

for another thirty seconds. Then people started appearing. "Regular speed now, please."

"Yes, sir."

"You watch, too." Boris studied the faces, waiting for the tall, slim woman to appear. He almost missed her under a baseball cap. "There. Can you follow her?"

The man nodded and pushed a button. The target walked down the hall, an overnight bag over her shoulder. The security officer kept pushing buttons, following her to ground transportation. She crossed the lanes of traffic and entered an Avis office.

"Well?"

"Sorry, we don't have cameras in the rental car offices."

Boris scrubbed at his forehead with his hand. "Show me everything along that strip."

The wall full of monitors lit up with various angles of the rental car offices and city bus stops.

"Slow it down a bit." Boris got up and stood back, keeping his hand on his gun.

"Now, back it up about ten seconds." Boris blurred his eyes so he could watch multiple angles, looking for a baseball cap, the beige jacket she wore. Nothing.

"How about inside the parking garage?"

The man pushed more buttons and again multiple angles of the parked cars flooded the screens.

"Just the elevators and stairs. You can speed it up again."

Half the screens went blank. He watched intently. People came and went for about five minutes, then a light-skinned black woman dressed in a maid's uniform with a tight bun in the back of her neck walked out of the stairwell on the top floor. She'd shed the cap. "Can you magnify her face?"

"A little." He spun a dial on the console and the image focused in.

"There she is."

The security man's face lit up. He seemed to be enjoying the intrigue. "She's pretty."

"Some of the worst ones are."

The young man looked wistful.

"I'm in a hurry. Go back to the street view at this new timeline."

Boris watched as his target emerged from between two rental car companies and got on the #42 bus.

"Got'cha." He glanced at the security guy's name tag. "Thank you for your service, Ron. I'll mention your help to your supervisor."

"Uh, sure. What's your name?"

But Boris was already out the door. He should have killed the kid, but he hadn't let him get a good look at his face. Kept him facing forward most of the time. Still, Boris guessed he was getting soft in his old age.

He ran to his vehicle, punched in a map of the route for #42, and went after his target.

CHAPTER

# TWENTY

Rainey willed the bus to go faster. She worried she stuck out with only three other passengers on board, but she passed as a maid coming back from her shift in an airport hotel. Still, she wondered if she'd lost whoever was following her.

About halfway through the route, she rang the bell and got off at Alcazar St. She stepped into the shadows of some bushes, waiting to see if anybody was following the bus. Sure enough, a black SUV drove by and stayed behind the slow-moving bus rather than passing it. She punched the license plate number into her phone.

Walking over to the posted schedule, she saw another bus was due in fifteen minutes. Should she nick a car and drive down to the water? It would be fast, but would also leave breadcrumbs. Staying in the shadows, she waited and took a minute to check the New York Times website. No news about an attempted assassination. She checked the Washington Post. Again, nothing. They were keeping it all under wraps.

She pulled up the president's twitter feed. He was clueless enough to tweet about it. But all she found were lots of self-congratulations, lots of claims of bogus news.

"Corrupt media claims I will lose. Wrong."

"Moron Murray wants to steal your health insurance. Socialist. Bad."

"Leftist Gang in the House against Israel. Hate Jews."

He didn't have a clue the people who'd put him in office were now set to take him out. Plus whoever had hired her through Control.

She heard the bus rumbling toward her and stepped up to the stop. It pulled over for her with a squeal of hydraulic brakes and she got on, paid her fare, and picked a seat away from the lights. She tied a scarf on her head, which put her in mind of her grandmother. She'd ridden many buses back and forth to people's houses to clean and mind their children. She took out a compact and looked behind the bus. No black SUV. Good so far.

She was tempted to jump off at the stop before the Douglas Street Monorail Station, but it would add too many miles to her trip. She checked out the route from the station to her destination—Grove Key Marina. Just under two miles. The side streets would provide enough cover. If the first marina didn't work out, there were others in the area, including a sailing club.

Tightening her scarf, she hunched over as she left the bus, adding imaginary age to her frame. She took the overpass across the highway, forcing herself to walk at a slow pace, then headed over to Percival Avenue. Skipping up to Day Avenue, she felt safe to jog until she was within a couple of blocks of the water. She cut through the alleyways of a hotel and the Fresh Market where she entered a bathroom, stripped off her maid's uniform and pulled on a wetsuit. She wrapped her carry-on in a plastic bag with sealing clips to make it watertight.

Rainey headed toward the water, staying in the shadows. Nobody was around. Must be well after midnight. A dock appeared, well lit, stretching out toward dark water. The Dinner Key Marina just to the north shone in the bright lights, illuminating a big building, several guard stations, and lots of fence. A bit of a swim, but the smooth surface promised calm.

The smaller Grove Key Marina a touch further north seemed like a good bet, but was still well guarded. Perhaps she'd take a private boat from the sailing club to the south. Maybe she could find one that had been covered for the winter and wouldn't be missed. She'd make up her mind once she swam around a bit.

Rainey strapped the bag to her back and found a shadowed spot on the shore. She slipped into the water, walking until the sea came up to her knees. Then she submerged, only her head above the waterline like a seal. She'd expected bathtub warm, but the water was cool enough to give her an initial chill. She started to swim, setting a good pace. The exercise, the dark water with some stars shining through the lights, relaxed her. She swam out to the bevy of boats anchored off the sailing club and treaded water, looking for a likely prospect. Best to take something from the middle, she thought. Less chance of being missed.

Something brushed her leg beneath the water. She held perfectly still.

Nothing happened.

Rainey allowed her legs to rise and floated for a full minute, making small movements like fish fins with her hands.

Nothing disturbed the surface.

Deciding she was safe, Rainey dogpaddled between two small sloops, then swam between a sloop and a cutter. Larger boats sat in the third row, rocking in the small swells. She swam up to what she thought was a yawl, all tarped for the winter. This one might be difficult to handle and certainly hard to hide.

Music floated over the water, coming from one of the boats. Then voices reached her, a man and woman. Sounds over water were notoriously difficult to spot. She held onto the side of the yawl she'd been considering, waiting.

"Want to take her out?" a man asked.

"I'd rather take this out." The woman gave a husky laugh.

"All right, baby."

The couple seemed absorbed in themselves, so Rainey set off again, swimming into the drift of boats, looking for something small and easy to handle. In the next row, she found a perfect racing sloop, about thirty-five feet. She swam around the boat, loosening the cover, then crawled underneath and pulled herself up into the hull. She dragged the cover back and stowed it in a corner. Luckily, the sails were folded in a box next to the mast. She made quick work of attaching them and weighed anchor.

The high tide was pulling out, so she let the boat drift out, then pulled the string on the old-fashioned motor and steered out of the marina. Once she was away from the other boats, she hoisted the mainsail. It caught the breeze and billowed out. The little boat picked up speed, riding the swells easily.

Rainey checked the map on her phone, then activated her security, then the locator. Once she cleared the barrier islands and hit the open ocean, the swells turned to waves. She raised the headsail and headed toward Marathon. She hoped the wind would pick up so she could get up to speed and make the trip in six or seven hours, just as the sun rose. Any longer and she risked being spotted.

Rainey settled in, moving the sail billowing above her to make the most of the breeze. She was far enough away from shore to avoid any obstructions. She'd checked the map carefully on the plane. About half an hour into the trip, the wind picked up and she flew over the dark water, keeping a sharp lookout for boat lights and buoys. Hopefully, nobody was crazy enough to be on this side of the islands so late at night.

Relaxing as she got used to the boat and the speed, she let herself watch the spectacular display of the Milky Way, a river of light above her head. A few hours into the sail, the sea lit up with phosphorescent plankton, as if some stars had fallen and lit the ocean as they sank. Later, a thunderstorm far enough away not to be a threat offered an awe-inspiring display of strikes that lit the clouds and ocean beneath them.

Her father had taken her sailing once for her seventh birthday. Her mother packed sandwiches in a basket. They took the Long Island Railway from Grand Central Station and then a taxi out to the marina. That had been treat enough for her, but then they'd rented a small sailboat and her father had taken them on a little tour of the large mansions dotting the shores.

He talked about his childhood in Bombay, before it had reclaimed its former name of Mumbai, how he and his two older brothers had begged and begged until their father let them learn to sail from an old friend of the family.

"He was a crusty old fisherman. The boat barely fit us all and stank of fish, but we were ecstatic. We stayed out all day, not even minding as the fish piled up around us."

Mother smiled as he talked, his eyes shining.

"I rowed in college, but those rivers could never replace the sea," he said.

"Let's stop and eat our lunch," Mother said.

Her father trimmed the sails, a magical process, and they slowed to a glide. He dropped anchor and Mother revealed her magical creations. Later in the city, they stopped for cake at Rainey's favorite bakery.

Thinking of her parents, her eyes filled. The Army had told them she'd died, and her body could not be recovered. She hadn't revealed herself to them. It would be a huge security risk. That was one thing she could never forgive those fellow soldiers for.

The riggings started to flap in the wind. Rainey noticed the stars were now obscured by clouds. The storm had turned toward her. The winds picked up and the smooth swells grew steeper. She trimmed the sails and took a firm hold on the tiller. The dark water surged around her, lapping over the sides and drenching her. Lightning strikes continued and the thunder boomed close. She held on, wet and shivering, steering straight into the whitecaps.

After an hour of struggle, the storm turned just before it broke over her full force, heading southwest. The water calmed. Rainey got her phone out again and took a reading. She hadn't been blown off course by much and the tail-winds of the storm would help her make up the time. She loosed the sails.

The sky cleared and a sliver of moon sat in the west, a star almost caught in its curve. The deep midnight sky turned to purple, then began to lighten into blue. The shore was a dark smudge on the horizon. Rainey headed closer to the islands and checked her position again. An hour out. She just might make it unobserved.

Her stomach growled. She'd eaten her last protein bar a couple of hours ago. Yesterday, she'd been too busy chasing down the Albanian and escaping whoever was on her tail to eat. Maybe it would be good to arrive hungry. It would show in her eyes and perhaps the house staff supervisor would take pity on her. But then again, this was Earl's staff she was talking about. She drank another third of her last bottle of water and watched for navigation buoys.

Ibis Island appeared in the distance and Rainey checked her location again. The hidden bay she'd found on Google maps was on the west side, just around the southern tip. Rainey tacked around the island, leaving the huge orange ball peeking over the horizon, and trimmed the sails when the wind picked up. The boat glided along. She spotted the spit of land that marked the small bay, grabbed the tiller, and steered toward it. This side of the island still lay in shadows.

She pulled close to shore just around the edge of the spit under the low hanging limb of a mangrove tree. The boat would be less visible here. She dropped anchor and with the splash, birds erupted from the trees. Rainey drew the cover over the boat, grabbed her bag and slipped into the water. She swam to shore, careful of shoals.

The rocky beach made footing uncertain. She picked her way over to a small stream that trickled over smaller stones and then flattened out to soak into the sand and join the sea. She stripped off her wet suit and washed in the fresh water, then unwrapped the black plastic and pulled out her bag. The plastic had done its work. The bag was dry. She dressed in clean underwear, shorts, and shirt. She pulled on a pair of sneakers, hid her wet suit under an overhanging rock, shouldered her bag, and set off.

She walked the beach looking for a path to the interior

of the island, careful of the stones. A sprained ankle would slow down her assignment or even get her killed. She ducked under a tangle of low-hanging mangrove trees and came out on a white sand beach. Up ahead, a footpath led from the water through the shrubs and sea grass. Rainey took it and walked through another grove of trees that gave out onto a wide dirt road. She checked her compass and headed north.

Insects buzzed around her head in the growing heat of the sun. The trees surrounded the path with wildflowers peeking through the thick growth on the sides of the track, vying for more sun. A flash of green caught her eye. Then the green settled on a limb and resolved into a parrot.

"Good morning," she whispered

The bird peered at her out of one eye, then the other, squawked, then decided she was acceptable. A bird so bright must be a male. He began to groom his wings. The waves from the nearby beach lulled her into a smooth pace. Soon the path turned eastward, and the ground rose. Rainey walked up the hill. At the top, the trees thinned and ahead of her she saw the sprawl of Earl's complex. She dropped to her knees to study it.

The main lodge looked to be about four stories with wrap-around porches. The sun-bleached wood had been left natural and made a pleasing contrast with the green lawns and smaller cottages spread along the south side of the complex. A series of pools almost surrounded the complex and a white sand beach stretched in front with a pier and marina at the far south of the property. A lavish private house stood proudly to the north of the resort. What surprised her most were the solar panels. She sheltered under a fichus tree and took out her binoculars. The panels seemed to be connected by thick wires to a shed on the north side of the lodge. Probably a battery storage system.

"Earl, you sneaky bastard. You do believe in climate change," she said. She'd always suspected half his political opinions were a show to please his base. The other half she was now certain were imported.

Rainey stowed her binoculars, shouldered her pack, and walked down the hill, staying behind a row of ornamental bushes that hid a kitchen garden to her right. A patch of unsheltered ground stretched between the bushes and the back of the lodge. She looked for people. No security. Seemed a bit lax, but then who could sneak onto an island this isolated? She could, obviously, but would the Secret Service worry about it? Just as she was about to step out from the bush, two guards dressed in the suits of the Secret Service walked around the corner of the lodge. They strolled along, their gaze sweeping over the grounds.

Rainey crouched down and waited. They walked the length of the lodge, then headed toward the cottages. She waited another minute, then started toward the house.

Something stung her neck. She slapped at what she thought was a bee, but instead found a small dart sticking in her skin.

"Damn it," she said, then just caught herself against the trunk of the tree and slipped down to the ground, losing consciousness.

# TWENTY-ONE

Rainey swam up from a dark sleep. She tried to swallow, but her mouth was dry as wood shavings. She recognized the faint metallic taste. Somebody had drugged her. Taken her somewhere.

The light beyond her eyelids told her it might be late afternoon. The rancid cloth stuffed in her mouth almost made her gag, but she controlled her response.

She focused on the sounds around her, eyes still closed, body stock still.

A gang of starlings made an uproar as they sang to each other in trees nearby. At the nunnery, a huge flock had gathered like this in the afternoon, sharing the news of the day. The nuns called it their satsang.

Now she was sure of the time. She'd been out a good part of the day.

In the near distance, voices called to each other, but she couldn't make out any words. An engine started up, maybe a boat. In the far distance, the gentle lull of waves.

No breeze blew over her, so she knew she was inside. She listened for any movement.

Nothing.

She wiggled her fingers, then tried to move her wrists. Tied tight. Same with her ankles.

"I know you're awake." The Russian accent said it all.

For a second, Rainey thought she'd play possum, but her small movements had already given her away. She tried to move her head, but it was strapped down. She opened her eyes, squinting against the light from the window, and studied her host next to her.

Close cropped dark hair barely covered his round head. His generous nose started out straight, then veered to the left. Black pants and work boots. The top of an inked skull peaked above the neck of his dark t-shirt. A killer, if she remembered her Russian tattoos correctly.

"Sleep well?" He had the rough voice of a life-long smoker.

Rainey tried to move, but straps across her chest, hips, and knees stopped her.

"You must eat clean. No drugs or booze? That dose really knocked you out."

He pulled the gag out of her mouth and Rainey took deep breaths, appreciating the clean sea air.

"What time is it?" she asked. Her tongue was thick like a wad of cotton.

"Afternoon."

"Can I have some water, please sir?" Rainey put on her southern drawl, compliments of her mother.

Her captor snorted at her courtesy. "You'll have plenty soon."

He tilted his head toward several buckets brimming with water and a towel. Rainey followed his glaze.

*Oh, joy,* she thought.

She pulled against her straps and felt the table she was tied to give just a bit. Good news.

"You are a bit of a mystery, little one."

"A mystery?"

"SVR didn't know about you. They do now." His laugh had a cruel edge.

Control would have to get 7R4C3R to hack in and erase it again.

"How'd you get the drop on the Albanian, huh?"

"Who?"

This earned her a slap. She took a deep breath and pushed out the pain with her exhale.

"The Albanian. The man you killed in Atlanta."

"I ain't been in Atlanta. Came here to get work." She forced hysteria into her voice, trying to divert his attention as she probed the straps for a weakness.

"Work? You killed a world famous assassin."

"No, sir. I live over to Marathon. Heard they was hiring for a big party."

Boris leaned over her. "You died in Afghanistan. You are a ghost."

"Naw, you got the wrong girl." Rainey tried to scramble away from him, but the straps only allowed her to squirm.

"You're special forces."

"What'chu talking 'bout?"

"The question of the day is who sent you?" he continued, ignoring her objections.

"I came here to work the party."

"We'll see." The Russian put a towel over her face. "Here's your water, doll."

Even though Rainey had been trained to withstand torture, the sensation of drowning usually sent her into a panic after the eighth or ninth bucket. It was a weakness she hadn't conquered yet, so she'd concocted a story to tell to stop waterboarding.

After the third bucket, she sputtered and spit out water. Once she could speak, she dropped the accent and said, "No more. Please, I'll tell you."

"Women," the man said in disgust.

"I'm on contract. I work for the Brits."

"You're an American. Just listen to you."

"A British detail found me in Afghanistan. Saved my life. The Americans tried to kill me." She added some venom to her voice.

He studied her for a minute. "Too easy." He picked up another bucket and started slowly pouring water over the towel covering her mouth and nose.

She held her breath as long as she could, squirming under the deluge, trying to turn her face away, if only a millimeter. But finally her lungs burned and she gasped for air. Instead water filled her throat and flooded her lungs. Her vision dimmed and just at the last moment, the water stopped.

The man turned her head to the side.

She spit out water and coughed, trying to clear her airways. Her head ached.

"Who sent you?"

"I told you," Rainey said in a voice rough from coughing up water.

Boris grabbed a handful of hair and pulled her head toward him. "Tell me again."

"I work for the Brits. Code name Dandelion." 7R4C3R had embedded a link into British Intelligence. Once he clicked on the name, he'd be taken to a mirror site that confirmed her identity. She had no idea how it worked, but was confident in 7R4C3R's expertise.

"How come you're giving in so easy, huh?"

"I almost drown when I was a kid. Please, I can't take this."

He pulled on her straps, tightening them, then stuffed the rag back in her mouth. "I'm going to check out your story."

Boris walked out of the room. The lock clicked behind him. Rainey cursed the Russian for tightening the straps again, but controlled her anger. She pulled the thickest part of her hand into the strap and made a fist. The strap gave a bit. Rainey did this a few times until she'd loosened the strap enough to flatten her hand. She bit her lip to stop herself from making a sound and dislocated her thumb by pushing against the table. She pulled her hand out, scrapping against the metal of the buckle, then jerked her thumb back in place. Once free, she unbuckled her other hand, then undid all her restraints.

"All right, Miss Dandelion—"

Rainey grabbed a cheap gold floor lamp and swung the base at the Russian as he walked through the door.

He ducked, but the base caught him on the temple. "Bitch." He barreled toward her, hitting her in the gut with his full weight.

Rainey stuck out her elbow as they went down. The point dug into his gut, pushing him slightly to the left. She thrashed around and got some room, then pushed off him.

The Russian grappled with her, but Rainey slipped out of his grip.

She got to her feet and took a step toward the door. He grabbed her ankle and brought her down. She rolled and jerked her foot from his grip, came back up, and bolted to the door.

She rushed toward the outside, the Russian so close she

could feel his breath. A pistol lay on the kitchen counter near the door.

The Russian grabbed for it, but his fingers closed on her shirt.

Rainey snatched the gun, turned and fired. The sound was suppressed.

*Thank God*, she thought. She hadn't had time to check.

The shot hit the Russian in the gut. He fell back and she headed for the door, but he got his legs under his body and pushed up. He lunged at her, grabbing her around the waist.

Rainey kicked him in his gut and more blood spurted out.

He pulled a knife from his boot and slashed at the tendons in her ankle.

Rainey jumped back, aimed, and got him with a head shot. His eyes went wide, then with his last breath, a look of astonishment briefly passed over his face and peace replaced his grimace.

"Not as bad as you expected, huh?" she whispered.

She paused for a moment to honor his passing, then looked at the pistol. It was a Russian made Makarov. She pushed it into the back of her jeans and checked her clothes for blood. They were clear.

She pulled a curtain back and looked outside. Nobody was rushing to see what had happened. Fuchsia bushes in a riot of magenta hung over the walkway. Good cover.

She found her bag thrown on a chair next to the window. She grabbed it and went outside. Her shirt was soaked with water and sweat, but a few minutes in this heat should remedy that.

Rainey walked toward the main building, forcing down her urge to run. Time to get a job for the party.

# CHAPTER
# TWENTY-TWO

Grant stood in the bow of Earl's Marquis LY 650 yacht watching for other boats that got too close, but the ocean was empty around them. Grant's eyes watered in the bright sun. He'd forgotten to pack sunglasses.

With the Coast Guard accompanying the president, he could relax. They'd flown from Dobbins near Atlanta into Homestead Airforce Base mid-morning, but rather than taking a chopper to the island, Earl had insisted on using his new yacht. Morton had turned an amusing shade of deep red.

This new model hadn't been released to the public yet. Grant didn't know how Earl had gotten his mitts on it, but could guess it was a bribe—or a gift in exchange for Earl's support, as the corporate heads thought of it. So, naturally he wanted to show it off to the party guests. Sixty-five feet of luxury, it boasted three lavish staterooms along with several multi-purpose recreation and lounge areas. A mix of bronze and black, it cut through the deep blue of the water, sleek as a bottle-nosed dolphin.

Grant braced against the railing in front and enjoyed the ocean air, not minding the occasional dousing as they cut through the waves. They passed emerald isles with stretches of white sand. The resorts crowded up close to the beaches on the bigger islands, dripping with wrap-around pools and balconies. The boat drifted close to a small island where the sparkling blue of the deeper channel turned turquoise closer to the shore. Grant looked forward to relaxing before their next round of rallies, going for a swim, watching the women in their bikinis or lack thereof. It was a private island, after all.

The yacht navigated around a wild shore filled with mangrove trees and sudden huge flowers he had no name for. They headed up the northeast side of the island and Grant realized this was Earl's place, the famed Ibis Isle. He climbed back down into the main lounge and waited for the boat to dock. But instead they stopped close to shore and dropped anchor. All the better to be seen by his guests.

A flotilla of motorboats headed out toward the yacht. Earl and a few Ken Dolls disembarked first. Red Sky left soon after, all crowded together. Their boat slid in parallel to the dock and Brad got out first, standing and admiring the main lodge and its archipelago of small cottages as if he owned the joint. Grant, Derrick, and George clambered out behind him.

"Your luggage will be delivered to your rooms," the pilot said before turning the boat back toward the yacht.

A young woman with a clipboard approached them, her blond hair pulled back in a ponytail. She wore blue slacks and a white shirt with a round pin featuring an Ibis bird and the name of the island in a circle around it.

She handed each of them a cold glass of mango and peach juice. "To refresh you from your travels."

"Thanks," Grant said. He took a long drink and was disappointed to find no alcohol in it. Still, it hit the spot.

"You may get your room assignments at the desk in the main lobby along with your keys," she said. "Please let the staff know how we can make your stay more enjoyable."

Grant followed his compatriots across the lush lawn and up three wide steps. The lobby floor was stone with streaks of brown and a deep blue that made it look like a rocky beach. The ceiling opened to the floors above, with wood railings lining the outer hallways. Large palms and tropical flowers in the center stretched up toward skylights. A blue parakeet sat on a branch studying the group.

Earl stood in the middle of the lobby talking loudly to a group of older men. "I'm winning that money back this time, Jones. I'll see you on the course tomorrow morning."

"Right you are, Mr. President."

"They have a golf course?" Grant asked.

"A few holes, I think," George said.

"The Ken Dolls are on tonight, so we have the night off," Brad said.

"Excellent," Derrick said, drawing the word out.

"Let's go to the dining room first. I'm starved," Brad said.

The line at the reception desk confirmed the decision to eat first. They'd missed lunch and it was already close to three o'clock.

"Meet you there." Grant headed to the men's room. They'd been on the boat quite a while.

When he got to the dining room, Brad shouted out, "I ordered a huge meat lover's pizza. Salad bar over there. Gotta eat those greens."

A long table stood against the wall filled with a variety

of lettuce and spinach, assorted vegetables, pasta salads, seafood salads, and dressings.

"Looks good. Grab me a beer, would you?" Grant said.

"Sure thing," Derrick said.

Grant stepped over and started to fill his plate with lobster and crab legs.

*Fuck greens*, he thought.

He sat at the table and took a long pull of beer. Looking up, he caught a glimpse of a woman walking across the lobby. Her hair was pulled back in a tight chignon at the base of her skull, but a few strands had escaped and now hung in loose curls. Something about her profile, the way she moved, reminded him of Madison.

He shook his head. *You're just imagining things.*

## CHAPTER

# TWENTY-THREE

Rainey spotted the group in the dining room when she crossed the lobby. A chill spread through her when she saw Brad's face, a flash of it twisted in pleasure while she pulled in vain against the stakes she was tied spread-eagle to. She shook her head against the memory. Another life—literally. His cronies sat around him, just like a pride of young lions.

She wondered if Grant had kept his word. Just her luck they'd joined Red Sky and been given this assignment. She'd need to stay sharp to avoid them. Being a maid wouldn't give her full access to the lodge, so she'd decided to join the "massage staff." That way she could go anywhere without much question.

She ducked into the women's room and checked herself in the mirror. Passable. Stood in front of the dryer for a minute and pulled her shirt out in front of the hot air to get the rest of the water off. She went back out into the hall and heard footsteps. A security guard passed and nodded to her. She gave him a smile. Pushing open the glass doors to the main staff office behind reception, Rainey stepped in.

A young woman with eye shadow that mimicked a parrot's wings glanced up and smiled. "How may I help you?"

Rainey paused a second too long, recovering from the surprise of the garish makeup and seeing her former killers outside. She pulled her cover story firmly around her.

"Yes, ma'am, my boss over to Key Largo said I should come work the party."

"And who is your boss?"

"Diamond Carter, ma'am. She runs—"

"Yes, we know who Diamond is. Your name?"

"Laila Jones, ma'am."

"Take a seat, please."

Rainey sat out of view of the glass door to the main office. She picked up a fashion magazine and started thumbing through it, feigning interest.

A harried, middle-aged woman rushed through a door to the back of the office and glanced around. Rainey stood and the woman looked her up and down. A frown formed on her face. "Laila?"

"Yes, ma'am. Massage therapist."

The woman raised an eyebrow. "I hope you can do more than that."

"Oh, yes ma'am. I understand the job."

The woman's gaze fell to her hands.

"I keep them short for the massage."

"Uh, hu." She still looked skeptical.

"I clean up real nice, ma'am. I didn't want to get all gussied up before the boat ride over with the wind and all."

She eyed Rainey. "What's Diamond's code word for trouble?"

"Tofu, ma'am." A Google search had turned this up on a

few women's Facebook pages. It amazed her how indiscreet people's posts were.

The woman gave a crisp nod. "Well, if you work for Diamond, I guess we can give you a try."

Rainey dipped her knees like she was in front of royalty. "Oh, thank you, ma'am. I can't tell you how much this means to me. My momma, she's sick and—"

"Yes, yes." The woman waved her hand in a dismissive gesture and turned to the receptionist. "Call Candi to take care of her."

The receptionist picked up the phone and pushed a button.

"Candi will get you all fixed up," the manager said to Rainey. "We're twenty-four seven the whole time Mr. Earl is in residence."

"Yes, ma'am."

She turned on her mid-level black pumps and marched back through the door she'd come through.

First obstacle down.

A few minutes later, Candi bustled into the staff office, the scent of gardenia coming with her. She led Rainey up the staff stairs to a big room that looked like the working girls' lounge. Make-up stands lined one wall in a long row. A kitchenette with two round tables filled the other side. Some sleeping spaces came next. In the back, clothes hung on racks, everything from tennis outfits and cheerleader outfits to nurses' uniforms. She caught a glimpse of satin behind these.

"Let's see." Candi stopped in front of one of the mirrored stands and turned Rainey's face this way and that, studying her. Then she grabbed her chin and tilted her face to the light. Her fingers traced the bruise Dushku had left on her right cheek. "We can cover that," Candi murmured, not asking or caring how she'd come by it.

The madam took a step back and studied Rainey's body. "I think we'll put you in black tights with this slinky, silver top. Lacy black bra."

"Beautiful."

"But you need a shower. In the back. Once you're dressed, pick up this house phone and dial 69 for me," she said without a hint of irony, "and I'll check your make-up.

"Yes, ma'am."

"And please don't call me ma'am. Makes me feel old." She winkled her nose and headed out.

Rainey picked out a locker in a shadowed corner and threw her bag and clothes inside, then punched in a series of numbers to secure it. She took her time in the shower, taking full advantage of all the jets designed to hit every square inch of her body. The products were a bit too perfumed for her taste, but she lathered up and then leaned into the pulsing streams of water, relaxing the knots of tension.

Her ribs had started to ache. She probed each one, winced when she poked the last one on the right. They all hurt, but nothing seemed broken. Her side would turn colors, but she didn't expect to be taking off the slinky, silver top she'd been assigned to wear.

She dried off with a deep tufted blue towel complete with the Ibis Isle logo—they didn't skimp on the help here. She chose a lavender body lotion, slathered herself in it as if it were protective armor, then slipped into her uniform. Rainey sat in front of one of the make-up tables and gently spread foundation over her bruise, then evened out the rest of her face. A bit of mascara and faint smoke eyeshadow, and she felt ready. She dialed Candi.

Five minutes later, Candi walked in, her floral perfume filling the room once again. Something about it reminded Rainey of her grandmother.

"Let's have a look at you. A bit too subtle, I think." She picked up a brush and rouge pot and put spots of color on Rainey's cheeks. Then she selected a small jar of silver that turned out to be glitter. "Close your eyes."

Rainey suffered her ministrations. With Candi leaning so close, she recognized the perfume and decided to win her over a little. "Is that Jungle Gardenia you wearing?"

"Why, yes, it is." Candi's voice softened.

"I just love that scent. Can't hardly find it now."

"Found it in a catalog that sells old-fashioned things." She huffed when she said these last words. "Stuff that isn't made anymore. But some things are classics."

"I agree."

Candi blew across her eyelids. "Now look at yourself."

Rainey squinted, worried she'd get glitter in her eyes, but Candi had blown away any stray flecks. "My goodness." She thought she resembled an iridescent hoot owl.

"You like?"

"It's amazing. I never thought I could look so nice. Thank you, ma—Candi."

"You're welcome." She fluffed up Rainey's hair, twisting a few strands around her finger to tighten the curl. "Perfect. Now, go walk around the lobby and outside. Go flirt." She gave her a proprietary pat on the butt as Rainey walked by.

Second obstacle down.

Rainey sauntered out into the lobby and earned a few leers from the executives and lobbyists checking in. She walked around the building toward the cottages, looking for any activity. Just the normal flurry of people milling around. Nobody seemed alarmed. But then, this was Earl's property after all. Maybe dead bodies weren't that unusual.

She circled around and went back to the dressing room, now thankfully empty. Her locker hadn't been disturbed. She opened it and unzipped her bag. The Makarov lay next to her phone in the middle of her clothes. She pulled it out and checked the rounds. Eight left. That matched her memory.

Maybe she could lift another weapon from a lodge security guard. These Makarov's took an odd sized bullet. Rainey stuffed the pistol into the back of her tights. Her loose top covered it nicely. She grabbed her phone, went into a bathroom stall, and punched in a code to secure it. Time to go outside.

The path to the cottages still seemed quiet. She walked down the path toward the golf course and once she was far enough away from the lodge, veered into the trees. She found a large, flat rock and sat down. Rainey pulled her phone from the deep pocket in the tunic she'd been given and found a condom. Disgusted, she tossed this into the woods behind her.

She opened the web. Navigating to the lodge website, she familiarized herself with the layout. Finding a backdoor to the staff message board, she silently thanked 7R4C3R for teaching her what he called Hacking 101. Earl's home stood up the beach from the lodge, a magnificent three-storied house with a furnished basement that resembled a cruise ship with a balcony running all around offering views of the Atlantic from all sides. She found the listing from a few years ago on Zillow. Why nobody had taken this down was a mystery. She scrolled through photos.

A pool stretched in the back under the sun, but also reached into the downstairs under the balcony, providing shade and privacy. This extended into a spa with hot tubs and two saunas. Also, lots of entrances. Inside, a long bar stood in front of a theatre room. The kitchen was downstairs in the back—arranged like the old houses of England where only servants cooked. More entrances.

On the main floor, a large dining area in the center was surrounded by equally spacious living rooms. More windows and doors. The second floor held bedrooms, each master sized with doors to the porches. On the ends were extra-large suites. Earl's domain was the top floor with an enormous bedroom, even larger bath, and lounge area plus office, all with huge windows and doors to the balcony. She suspected he kept this to himself.

Piece of cake to get in.

Except for the Secret Service. She wasn't worried about Red Sky. But they were here, and she'd need a better disguise. Good thing it was Halloween.

# TWENTY-FOUR

G rant's earpiece crackled to life. "Red Sky, report to the path to the cottages. We have a situation."

He'd expected it to be Brad calling them, but was surprised when he recognized the voice of John Morton, head of the Secret Service team here.

"Sorry, babe." He pointed to his ear. "Duty calls."

"Aw, will you come back?" She pushed her lips out in a sexy pout and lay back on a lounge chair. They were beside one of the pools enjoying the sunset, and Grant had just ordered some concoction with rum, tamarind, passionfruit, and lime juice. He loved to experiment.

"You bet I will. You stay warm and keep my drink cold." Grant leaned over and kissed her, then took off at a trot.

As he rounded the corner of the main lodge, he found Brad and George waiting. Derrick appeared half a minute later, still tucking in his shirt.

"Dipping your wick?" Brad asked. He didn't wait for an answer. "This way."

Grant and the rest of the team ran behind Brad down the row of cottages, some of which were hardly cottages, but two-story luxury houses. A group of Secret Service and lodge security clustered around the outside of the last cabin. Grant noted there were no local authorities, no police. He supposed the Secret Service was official, though. They stopped at the edge of the group.

"Who found him?" Morton was talking to the head of lodge security. Grant had been introduced to him when they first arrived, but he didn't remember his name.

"The maid." The man gestured toward a woman in a cleaning uniform who stood slightly away from the group, arms wrapped around herself. It was clear she'd been crying.

"Anybody else been in there?" Morton asked.

"I went in," the security man said.

"And?"

"A couple of my men."

"Did you touch anything?"

"Uh," the man's face fell as he realized his mistake. "Well, yes."

A deep sigh issued from Morton. "Great, now we've got a bunch of fingerprints and footprints to deal with."

"Sorry." He studied his shoe.

"I'm going in to examine the scene. You keep everybody else out. And don't talk to the guests or staff. This is a need-to-know situation."

"Yes, sir."

Morton pointed at his cluster of agents standing on the sidewalk. "And who's on Tycoon?"

"Ralph, sir."

He gave them a look. Two men peeled off and jogged to the lodge. Morton entered the cottage and closed the door behind him.

Brad pushed his way to the front of the group. Grant followed along with the other two Red Sky men.

"What happened, Julio?" Derrick asked. Leave it to Derrick to know the security guy's name.

"Sorry, I can't say."

"Oh, come on. We're security. We're responsible for guarding the president, right alongside Mr. Morton in there."

Julio looked around at his men and a cluster of Secret Service men peering in the windows of the cottage. "Found a dead body," he muttered.

"Male or female?" Brad asked.

"Male."

"Who is it?"

Julio just shook his head.

Grant caught Derrick's eye and, with a jerk of his head, indicated he should follow him. Grant approached the maid who still stood alone, huddled beside a gardenia bush. "May we ask you a question?"

The woman shook her head. "No entiendo."

"¿Podemos hacerte una pregunta?" Derrick translated.

"Si, señor."

Derrick continued in Spanish, asking her what had happened and translating for Grant. She'd come in to clean, just like always, and found broken glass and some over-turned furniture. Then she saw him—a dead man lying in the doorway between the living room and the bedroom, a red dot in the middle of his forehead.

She started to cry.

Grant made what he hoped were comforting clucks and Derrick spoke to her gently, not bothering to translate. He handed her a handkerchief. She dried her eyes, then blew her nose.

She tried to hand it back, but Derrick waved it away.

"Gracias, señor."

"Ask her what else she noticed," Grant said.

Derrick translated, but she started to cry again. "Es muy importante, señora. Por favor, inténtalo." She nodded and squared her shoulders.

Derrick explained what she was saying. "She saw something that didn't make any sense."

He listened, then said. "Beyond the body in the bedroom there was a table with buckets all around it."

Grant sucked in his breath and the woman's eyes went wide.

Derrick encouraged her and she continued. After she stopped, he translated for Grant. "She says she saw lots of towels. Water all over the floor."

"Fucking—"

The woman crossed herself, muttering something Grant didn't understand.

Grant and Derrick stared at each other, then Derrick thanked her. She asked something and Derrick nodded. The maid walked to her cleaning cart just down from the front door and started pushing it away.

Once she was out of earshot, Derrick asked, "Who the fuck is water boarding somebody here?"

"Now we know why he's dead. Wonder who he had in there," Grant said.

"What did she say?" The two Red Sky agents turned to find one of the Ken Dolls had walked up behind them.

Grant raised his eyebrows, silently asking Derrick if they should share their intel.

"Come on, guys. We're in this together," the agent said.

"Just telling us how she found the body. Lots of broken glass. Furniture overturned."

"Anything else?"

They both shook their heads.

The agent relaxed his shoulders. "What do you think is going on?"

"Beats me, but hey, look at all these guests." Grant put a sarcastic twist on the last word. "They're all doing something illegal, if you ask me, except for the girls."

The agent snorted. "Trust me, prostitution is still illegal."

"Well, yeah." Grant flushed. "But it's not like we're going to arrest them, is it?"

Then he noticed a muscular Arab man dressed in a Henley t-shirt and golf pants standing in the middle of the group of men near the door. "Who's that?" He pointed with his chin.

The agent shifted his position slightly so he could get a look. "Must be one of the prince's men."

"As in Prince Burki?"

"That would be the one," the agent said.

"Where are the Russians?"

At that moment, Morton walked out the door and called Brad over. Grant and Derrick moved closer so they could hear. The agent followed.

"He's a Russian," Morton said under his breath.

"Well, we found them," Grant whispered to Derrick and the agent.

"An assassin by the look of his gear," Morton said.

"These fuckers aren't going to quit," Brad said.

"Quiet. We don't want to alert the lodge's security."

"Right."

"There was waterboarding equipment in the bedroom. Water everywhere."

The agent Grant and Derrick had been talking to snorted and gave them a look of disgust.

Grant shrugged.

"By the looks of it, he captured somebody. The question is who? All my men are accounted for," Brad said.

"Same here."

They both looked over at Julio.

"I'll ask him," Morton said. "We need to arrange for the body to be transported."

"Is that a good idea?" Brad asked. "I mean, word will get out."

"What do you expect me to do, throw him in the ocean?"

Brad shrugged.

"He'll wash up on some beach," Morton objected. "Somebody will find him. With two bullets in him, I might add. Then it will get in the papers. Besides, we don't do business that way."

"Can you ship him to D.C.?"

"I suppose, but I don't have the manpower to spare. Who was he waterboarding? Another spy? A third assassin?"

"We need reinforcements," Brad said.

# TWENTY-FIVE

R ainey headed back to the lodge and behind the kitchen saw three pigs roasting over an open fire. People in white aprons stood near them, turning the spits. She didn't get close enough to see if the pigs had apples in their mouths. She felt sorry that they'd lost their lives to the likes of Earl and company.

Rounding the corner of the lodge, she noticed the cluster of agents outside the last cottage.

*They found him.*

She watched the group from a distance. Lights started coming on around the lodge, making it easier to see their faces. Morton came out of the cottage and called someone over to him. They put their heads together. The man he was talking to looked up and she recognized him.

Brad Rogers. Why was Morton talking to the Red Sky leader?

Then she noticed Grant hanging close to the two leaders, eavesdropping for sure. Why did she keep running into them? Was there some unfinished business for her? Did she need to heal more emotionally so she didn't react to their presence? They weren't on her list. She wanted to be finished with them, and not in any lethal way.

The other agents milled around, then a team arrived with a stretcher and entered the cottage. She didn't wait around to watch the body being removed.

Security would get very tight now. She'd have to be extra careful. She'd thought about a mask earlier. It was a Halloween party after all. Rainey headed back to the women's lounge to pick out a costume—preferably one with more pockets.

She made it upstairs without running into any more Red Sky men or getting propositioned by a guest. Two women sat on the chairs near the snack area drinking coffee and smoking. Their garish outfits didn't match their slumped shoulders and tired expressions. She nodded to them and kept going toward the back to the rows of clothes.

She walked the aisle, amazed by how many costumes there were. She turned the corner from the golf and tennis clothes. Next came the make-believe outfits she'd seen before—cheerleaders, nurses, schoolteachers, Playboy bunnies. She shook her head at the amount of energy that was spent to satisfy men's sexual appetites. In the next aisle she found a row of ball gowns, her fingers running across silk and velvet, polyester and satin, sequined skirts with tight bodices.

Around another corner, she found what she was looking for. Here were gypsy dresses, ballerina outfits, leotards with fairy wings, gowns from different eras, animal outfits, costumes from movies and cartoons, a whole row of wigs. Wonder Woman held a certain appeal, but she needed something with more camouflage. She couldn't wear anything with a big skirt. A sailor outfit? No mask to match with this.

The next aisle stopped her in her tracks. Leather pants and halter tops, leather skirts, leather masks, and on the far wall hung whips and clubs, a cat o' nine tails. Leather, silk, and nylon straps. Harnesses and leashes. The ever-popular handcuffs took up a good amount of space. She picked up what looked like a massage tool, but the spikes were steel and sharp.

Next came wicker baskets filled with dildos of various sizes and colors. Some were two headed. Others had little bunnies or kittens in front of the main shaft. She came across another one she named Cerberus for its three heads, but her imagination failed her when it came to how it would be positioned. Then studded dildos with blunted spikes. She hoped these were used on the clients and not vice versa.

Some kind of chair hung from the ceiling. All the straps baffled her as much as Cerberus. The rest of the wall resembled equipment from a medieval torture chamber. She turned away with a shudder. Maybe she should pick a dominatrix outfit, but based on the extent of this collection, she'd be too much in demand to get her real job done. She needed something that would give her some camouflage or just blend in.

Returning to the fantasy aisle, she picked out a simple bodysuit with a skeleton on it, then a skull mask. Next she chose a generic black witch's cape with a hood. Back in the S&M aisle, she found a scythe hanging on the wall. She ran her finger along it, then winced. A small line of red rose on her finger. Good, a sharp edge. Near it, she found a sleek holster in black leather and removed the black, eight-inch dildo. The holster was perfect for her gun.

Rainey took the outfit back to the showers, washed off all the makeup Candi had so carefully applied, and slipped into her new costume. She opened her locker and retrieved the syringe, still safe in its plastic container, and stuffed it in her pocket. Then she belted the holster on under her cape and slid her gun into it. She gave the scythe a few test swipes, pleased with the balance. She secured her mask and walked toward the door.

"Oooh, the boys will shit themselves," one of the women said.

"That's the plan." She laughed with them.

Outside, she found the stars had come out and a waxing moon rose low over the water. She stepped into the shadows of the lodge for a moment just to soak it all in. She was likely to be busy the rest of the night.

In the trees at the back of the property, the silhouette of a great horned owl stood out against the sky. She hadn't realized these birds lived in the Keys. The raptor turned its head toward her. They stared at each other for a moment.

"Good hunting, my friend. May we both succeed tonight."

The owl gave a hoot as if in answer and lifted into the air on magnificent, silent wings.

Taking this as a good omen, Rainey went back into the lodge and started her hunt for President Charles Jefferson Earl.

# CHAPTER
# TWENTY-SIX

She found him sitting at a big table on a raised platform dressed in what was probably an Armani tux, but she couldn't be sure from her position against the wall. Round tables spread across the space filled with older men accompanied by younger women—mostly those hired by Candi by the looks of it.

Badawy Simman, the Egyptian Minister of Finance, sat with another man she thought was the Minister of Foreign Affairs. She couldn't recall his name. Egyptian military filled in the rest of the table along with their female companions. Close to the front a sea of keffiyeh head-dresses announced the Saudi delegation. Behind them, she recognized officials from the Arab Emirates.

On the opposite side but still at the front sat the Russian oligarchs—Matvei Kiselev, the man who ran Rosoil, the largest Russian oil and gas company. Other men dressed in more Armani suits sat around the table. Most likely other oligarchs or people high up in the industry.

Behind them a man with a forced smile nervously rubbed his hands together. She couldn't remember his name, but she knew the face from her research for this job. Ukraine. A liaison between Shark Energy and Med Stream, who controlled most of the pipelines serving Europe. He had reason to be nervous with the recent scandals. They should put his picture beside the definition of the cliché "between a rock and a hard place."

She recognized faces from other oil and gas companies, arms manufacturing, pharmaceuticals, tech giants, and the newest billionaires, a couple of CEOs from social media companies. At least Hughes had decided to get out of his infamous t-shirt and jeans in favor of, well, a t-shirt and jacket. The eldest of the Johnston family, owners of the largest box store in the world, looked distinctly uncomfortable with the scantily dressed women around the room, but their children and heirs fit right in.

This room would be a prime target for revolutionaries, but they didn't have the means to fire a missile into it. Rainey shook her head at the thought.

Candi's girls were in full costume as fairies, mermaids, and princesses in bright, translucent fabrics. What a contrast they made with the penguin black and white of the suits and flowing white thobes.

Earl stood, a bit wobbly on his feet, and held up his glass. The volume of the room went from deafening to simply boisterous. "My friends, my friends. Thank you for coming, and thank you most of all for your donations!"

Laugher and tepid cheers went up.

"We've accomplished many of our goals. Oil and gas rules again and the geo-political barriers are falling rapidly." He nodded his head toward the Saudis and Russians in particular.

"We've weakened our competition in Iraq and Iran. In due time, we will control it all and the oil will flow unimpeded. Soon, the Arctic will have melted, leaving her treasures vulnerable to our drills." He made a lewd gesture that turned Rainey's stomach.

A cheer went up at this rather ominous proclamation.

"Your profits are downright scandalous, Henry." He raised his glass to one of the pharmaceutical owners.

"Our military is the best equipped in the world." He nodded to another table. "In fact, we have surplus to sell."

"My opponent wants to split you up, Mr. Hughes." He put ironic emphasis on the Mr.

The social media giant raised his own glass in tribute.

Earl sounded more lucid talking to his donors than he did when he ranted at his rallies or on twitter. Was that all an act? Somehow Rainey didn't think so.

"But most of all, I saved all of you a shit load of money in taxes. To four more years. We'll finish what we started."

The room erupted in applause. Some banged on the table, knocking over a few water glasses. The rich shed their suave ways here at Ibis Isle.

"Death to the socialists," Earl shouted. Then he looked startled and pointed right at Rainey. "I see someone is prepared to finish them off."

Rainey froze until she remembered her mask. She recovered her composure and did a low, slow bow to him.

*You don't know how right you are*, she thought.

Many laughed, but she noticed Morton on the other side of the room speaking into his cuff. The Secret Service agent nearby started to move in her direction.

"Here's to One World Government," someone shouted. A roar of approval rose from the crowd. Many stood and held up their glasses.

Rainey drifted toward the exit nearest her.

Earl gestured toward someone behind the scene and

both service doors opened. Waiters in stark white carried out the three unfortunate pigs she'd seen earlier. They did indeed have apples stuffed in their mouths. Behind them, lines of servers carried platters and bowls of vegetables and potatoes. At the tables, corks slid from wine bottles. The chaos allowed her to escape.

Rainey headed out into the dark, wondering if she should change her costume. She'd enjoyed the irony of it all, but now she'd been seen. Maybe Wonder Woman after all. She'd find a mask.

# TWENTY-SEVEN

G rant stood in the corner, pissed he couldn't join in the party. He'd been sent to search the rooms one more time after the discovery of the body. The man had been Russian. Probably another assassin. Even though he'd been in that meeting with Egorov and Burki, he still wasn't sure why they wanted their puppet dead. They thought Earl hadn't delivered his end of the bargain, but he'd done some of it. What did they expect? He guessed they wanted someone with a more political savvy. Rumor had it the third-party candidate was a Russian asset, but he couldn't figure that either. He shrugged and wondered if any of that roast pig was left.

At any rate, now he had to stand guard with a growling stomach. It was close to midnight, the witching hour. The American CEOs had indulged in the holiday and now he was surrounded by vampires, ghosts, ghouls, and medieval kings.

Earl staggered around the lobby, his abnormally pale face flushed, shouting about how he would rule forever. He wore a Roman toga with a wreath of green on his head.

Probably laurel leaves. Grant thought he should have gone with a Dracula costume. It suited his natural complexion. He wondered if Earl had gotten any sleep yet. He didn't think so.

People leaned over the railings of the three stories, cheering him on. Most were flat-out drunk and had thrown away all inhibitions. Those few who didn't care to do so had retired to their rooms.

"If I catch these goddamn traitors who spread stories to Congress" –his face turned into a menacing snarl— "you know what we used to do in the old days when we were smart with spies and treason, right? We used to handle it a little differently than we do now."

"Death to the traitors," someone shouted. Others picked up the phrase and shouted it from the three tiers.

On the second tier, some man leaned a girl over the banister, threw her skirts over her head, and unzipped. He thrust into her and started shouting, "Earl, Earl, Earl," with each thrust.

A few feet away, another man grabbed a girl. He pushed her against the railing, tore off her panties, and threw them down to Earl, who snatched them from the air and waved them over his head.

"Impeached? Do I look impeached?" he shouted. He threw the panties to the crowd in the lobby like a stripper throwing her clothes out to the audience.

They roared their approval.

Another woman leaned over a couch in the lobby and pulled off her thong, slinging it up in the air with her spiked heel. Her date unzipped his pants.

*Damn*, Grant thought, *it's turning into a full-scale Roman orgy.*

Things were getting out of hand quickly. Anything

could happen in a situation like this. They'd already found two assassins. The third could use this chaos to slip up to Earl or take a shot from across the room. Grant knew he should do something to redirect the crowd, but the fire in his groin made it hard to think. It was a private lodge, after all, but still. It would be hard to keep Earl safe.

"Fuck Murray," Earl shouted. "Fuck the Speaker of the House. Bitch! Impeach me?"

A woman with a mask resembling the Speaker raised her skirts as if inviting Earl to do just that. He threw back his head and laughed, almost losing his balance.

"Everyone enjoy yourselves. Next week, we win!"

Earl gestured for a few men to follow him. Grant had seen a few of them hanging around the party in Atlanta. The group headed out the front door of the lodge and turned toward Earl's private house.

"Skeleton is on the move," Grant said into his mic, relieved Earl was moving to a more controlled environment.

"Roger that," three voices answered.

"Grant, you're on him," Brad's voice crackled into the earpiece. "Derrick, George, do another sweep of the cottages, then each floor again. I'm checking the staff lounges. The Ken Dolls are headed to the residence."

"When do we eat?" Grant asked.

"Grab a sandwich," came the answer. "And keep your wicks dry."

"Aw, man," Derrick complained in his ear.

"You're professionals. Act like it."

Rainey had been delayed changing her costume by a group men insisting she come up to their suite. By the time she escaped without inflicting bodily harm on them, the party had moved to the lodge lobby. She negotiated a path through the pack of yelling and jostling crowd. A woman sat on a red velvet couch in the middle of the lobby, her skirts thrown up, another between her knees servicing her. Men jostled for a view.

A good distraction. Nobody was looking at Rainey. She pushed through and made it to the back hallway, then up the stairs. She peeled off her mask, pushed open the dressing room lounge, and ran smack into Brad.

The color drained from his face and his mouth worked. "Madison?" he whispered.

Rainey grabbed the wire to his earpiece and yanked it out, pulling the mic with it. She dropped it to the floor and smashed it with her foot.

"But—"

She didn't have time for this. She punched him in the solar plexus, then followed with a chop to the neck. He went down.

She jumped over him and headed toward the back of the room, but he was suddenly up. He punched her in the kidney.

She crashed to the floor, rolled, and came up again. Crouched in fighting stance.

"Bitch, what the fuck?" Brad shouted. "You ain't no ghost."

"Don't make me kill you, Brad," she said.

"Kill me? I killed you."

The three women in the break room stared. One had a fork full of salad paused halfway to her mouth.

Rainey just shook her head.

"But you had no pulse."

"Didn't want to leave anybody to testify about the gang rape you organized?"

"Oh, shit," said a woman dressed in a purple scarf concoction.

Brad turned on her. "This ain't your business, bitch."

The woman stood up, her purple-bedecked body unfolding until she towered over Brad. She put her hands on her hips, the muscles in her arms bulging.

Rainey did a double take. This was no slight woman, but a drag queen with the build of a marine. Candi's brothel was well stocked.

The purple vision wagged her head, a long peacock feather on top waving incongruously. "What you say to me?"

Still recovering from her surprise, Rainey was unprepared for Brad's next move. He launched himself through the air and grabbed her by the throat. They fell and he planted a knee on each arm, pinning her. He squeezed.

"I've got you this time," he snarled.

Rainey rocked back and forth, trying to get up, but the bastard was heavy. She struggled, but couldn't get her arms free. Her vision started to narrow. She pulled her legs up, planted her feet, and started to buck.

"Yeah, baby. You want some?" Brad said.

"Oh, hell no," somebody said.

Rainey's vision went black. Then she heard a loud whack and the pressure on her neck loosened. She took a deep breath and sat up.

Brad lay on the floor unconscious.

The purple drag queen stood over him, a cast iron frying pan in her hand.

"Thank you," Rainey choked out.

"My pleasure."

A second woman wearing a luminescent negligee over a lacy bra and panties extended her hand. Rainey took it and pulled herself to her feet.

"Name's Trixie," the drag queen said. "This here's Trudy. Sometimes we work as a duo. Maria's over there." Trixie looked over her shoulder at the cowering Latina in the corner. "It's all right, honey. You can come out."

The woman crept closer.

"This here's Maria," Trixie said.

"Laila."

"He called you something else."

"Changed my name after—" Rainey gestured toward Brad.

The two women nodded in understanding.

"Pleasure to meet you all." Rainey shook their hands.

"What's this all about, honey?" Trixie asked.

"I served in Afghanistan with him. One night he and some of his buddies surprised me in my room. They drove me out to a spot in the desert, staked me out, and raped me."

"Oh, my God." Trudy patted Rainey's shoulder.

"He seemed surprised to find you alive," Trixie said, a question in her voice.

Rainey teared up, then shook her head against the surge of emotion. "They left me for dead."

"I see. And here you were serving your country."

She nodded, afraid if she spoke, she'd break down. She thought she'd resolved all this.

Brad moaned.

"What'chu wanna do?" Trixie asked.

Rainey looked at the clock on the wall. Ten minutes to midnight. "I've got a job."

"You all right? We could get Candi to send somebody else," Trudy suggested.

Rainey shook her head. "Has to be me."

Maria made a disgusted sound. "One of those, huh?"

Trixie didn't give Rainey a chance to answer. "If there's one thing I'm sick and tired of is women getting hurt by other soldiers in the military. They don't do nothin' about it neither."

"I know that's right," Trudy said.

"Let's give him a little taste of his own medicine," Trixie said. "You run along now, honey. We'll take care of this one."

Rainey studied Trixie's stern face, then looked at Trudy and Maria in turn. They looked a bit scared, but determined.

"I'd appreciate it."

"We got some time off. Need a little bit of our own entertainment," Trixie said.

"Just don't kill him," Rainey said.

Light broke out on Trixie's face. "Well, aren't you sweet." She pulled Rainey in for a hug.

"It's just—"

"Don't you worry, honey. We'll just make him wish he was dead."

Rainey smiled. She picked up her mask and scythe, then walked back out the door.

CHAPTER

# TWENTY-EIGHT

U pstairs in Earl's private house, a group of young girls had been gathered in two interconnected living rooms where they were eating from a lavish buffet. The atmosphere was more subdued than the lodge. The teens wore fairy wings, feathers in their hair, sequined shawls, and peacock-colored masks. Some dressed as the movie heroines they'd grown up watching, a few as the heroine from *Frozen,* some as the female scientist from Wakanda, and even a Buffy of all things.

Their nubile beauty and innocence was scented with a hint of curious sexuality—a tempting aphrodisiac. Stunned by this generous display of ingénues, powerful emotions warred inside Grant. He felt an overwhelming attraction coupled with a hint of guilt and an equally powerful desire to protect them. He turned his attention to the older women who accompanied them—fair game.

Drop-dead gorgeous models and actresses in their early twenties were dressed in slinky sequins, one in a leotard with Cat Woman mask, one as Greta Garbo, and two as Marilyn Monroe. They spoke in small groups around the room, painting a glamorous picture of their lives in New York or Hollywood, promising they'd get the girls in with their agents.

"Tonight is your first step," said one woman close to him. "Just play along."

Music played in the adjoining room and some people danced. Grant stood against the wall watching. Earl and his special entourage had gone downstairs to get cleaned up. They'd be up shortly, and the real action would start. Grant hadn't heard from his team. He assumed they'd cleared the floors in the lodge and gone off to play.

What were the odds of their being a third assassin after all? Astronomical. Yet, he thought he'd seen Madison when they first arrived. No, that was just his shock at encountering a live ghost in Atlanta. He resented having to stand guard when he knew the Skeleton was safe. Besides, he'd counted three Ken Dolls on his way into the house, one in the front, one in the back, and one downstairs. Shit, he deserved to party tonight of all nights.

He accepted a glass of champaigne from a circulating waiter and made his way over to the table of hors d'oeuvre. He scarfed three ham sandwich wedges, then loaded a plate with peeled shrimp and cocktail sauce, found a corner chair, and started on his bounty. He hadn't eaten since lunch. His eyes were on his mounded plate when the person dressed as the Angel of Death slipped through the door and up the stairs.

RAINEY FOUND a bathroom off the hall upstairs and went in, closing the door behind her. She was still a bit shaken by her encounter with Brad in the lodge. Her reaction revealed that she still had some residue from the trauma of that night. This surprised her considering the complete release that had come with the wash of light as she'd lifted up out of her body. Perhaps on her return she'd taken back remnants of the experience. She'd meditate. Maybe do that eye-tracking treatment for PTSD she'd heard so much about. Shed Brad and his group like a set of old, ragged clothes.

Trixie had been a delightful surprise. She wondered what they had in mind for her old platoon leader. She turned her attention to the task at hand.

The heavy tread of men's steps sounded downstairs. "The best part of the evening, gentlemen." It was Earl's voice.

Laughter followed, a complex mix of lust and malice overlaid with a sprinkle of guilt.

Rainey's stomach lit with anger.

The footsteps faded into silence. She waited five more seconds and nudged open the bathroom door. The hall was empty. Where might Earl's lady lair be? The corridor stretched on both sides, with a set of double doors on each end. Probably one of those.

She headed left at a trot passing six rooms on each side. The doors were closed. She reached the end of the hallway and tested the gold-plated knob. The door slid open on well-oiled hinges.

Two amber lamps gave off a soft glow. They stood on elaborate marble end tables on either side of an enormous bed, twice the size of a king. She circled, studying the leopard chaise lounge, the matching sofas facing each other. An eighty-six-inch monitor dominated one wall. Soft music played from the speakers and images of softly colored mandalas changed like a kaleidoscope in the clarity of an OELD display. In the bathroom, soft beige tiles were accented with a lapis blue strip at shoulder level.

Very elegant. In fact, too elegant for Earl. His taste ran toward the garish. Plus, there was nothing personal about this room. It felt like a hotel room for the richest customer. The suite on the other end of the house, then.

Just as Rainey opened the door, the hallway filled with the voices of men and girls. Damn it, they were coming up the stairs.

"You'll really love the rooms, girls," Earl said, his voice high and excited. "We've got something for everyone."

Rainey tiptoed up to a closet in the hall close by. Inside, she found cleaning equipment, plus just enough room to crouch. She closed the door just in time.

Earl's voice grew louder. "Here's the African safari room complete with the head of a lion my sons brought down." Now Earl's voice sound muffled. He must have bone into the room. "This is a genuine elephant tusk from the 11th century carved by Italian masters."

She heard little feminine sounds of appreciation.

"Don't get too rambunctious, Steve."

Rainey pushed the door open just a crack so she could see. The CEO of one of the pharmaceutical companies escorted a wide-eyed brunette, probably around fourteen, into the room. "We won't break anything, Mr. President."

"Who likes France? This is a replica of a room from Louis XIV's Palace of Versailles." Earl threw the door open so hard that it banged against the wall.

Several oohs and ahs issued from the group.

"Here's a medieval castle straight from the time of King Arthur. And across from it, something a bit more modern. The Roaring Twenties, complete with a whole closet of dresses—what do they call this style?"

"Art Deco, Mr. President?" someone offered.

Most of the girls pushed forward to see. The men stayed behind them, watching, eager. Rainey was pinned down.

The tour continued. "Who walks like an Egyptian?" Earl asked, doing an impression of the old dance that these girls did not remember.

Earl reeled off the list of theme rooms, his explanations growing shorter. A Chinese room. Indian. "Here's one from the Sixties, with tie-dye and lots of floor pillows, plus a hookah." Earl's voice was suggestive.

Rainey watched through the crack as two girls made their escape back down the stairs, but it seemed sadly that most were staying for the full experience. The group reached the end of the hall and Earl opened the double doors with a flourish. "An executive suite. Very exclusive."

An older Arab man went in with a redhead on his arm. Rainey could only see her back. So, Earl's playroom was on the other end of the hallway.

The group trooped past her hiding spot and Earl threw up his hands. "Go explore, girls. Find your dream room."

The girls went off in a pack, opening doors, exclaiming over their discoveries. The men followed, waiting for one of them to linger a bit too long. Rainey could make out the back of Earl's head, his black hair coiffed in a duck tail, tugging a young blonde behind him. He pulled her inside and the door closed.

She'd have to wait for the corridor to clear. She listened to the murmur of conversation. Ten more minutes passed.

Two more girls peeled off and ran down the stairway. They stood close enough for her to overhear.

"I don't care if I get a part in a picture. I just can't do this."

Her friend grabbed her hand. "Let's get out of here. It's safer downstairs."

*Good choice*, Rainey thought.

At last all the doors had closed. Some strains of music floated though one along with little squeals. Rainey opened the closet door and streaked down the hall. As she moved, she heard a muted scream. The double doors at the end were each decorated with elaborate borders and large E's carved in the middle.

She tried to turn the handle, but it didn't budge.

"No, Mr. President, please," she heard from behind the locked door.

"Don't be rude. You came in here with me."

Rainey looked around for something to force the lock. The hallway was clear. She fumbled in her pockets for her lock picks, but didn't find them. They must have fallen out in the struggle with Brad. She searched her hair and pockets, looking for a pin or a straight edge to stick into the lock.

Nothing.

She pulled the plastic container with the syringe out of her pocket. The top had cracked but the needle was still in tack. Thank heaven for small miracles. She couldn't risk it on the door, though.

"Please don't," the girl pleaded.

"I can do anything I want. I'm the King. King of America. King of Israel."

"No," came a loud shout.

"Oh, hold still. You know you came up here for this."

Rainey tried the door again, then pushed her shoulders against it. The sturdy wood held. Rainey swung the scythe down on the lock, but the door held.

Then the real screams started. High and shrill. The screams of a frightened child.

Rainey ran down the hall and picked up a rock statue of the Buddha. With a grunt, she lifted it and loped back as fast as she could.

"I apologize," she whispered to the Buddha, then swung the statue back and forth a few times, picking up momentum, then smashed into the knob.

It broke. She pushed the door open.

She was momentarily stunned by the gold—gold curtains, gold wallpaper, gold trimmed chairs, a gold dresser—all reflected by the mirrored ceiling. In front of her stood a massive bed surrounded by four oversized gold pillars elaborately carved. On the bed, a waif struggled against restraints, tears running down her mascara-streaked face. Earl stood naked beside her, pontificating. He shouted so loud that he had noticed her entrance.

"I'm going to win again. My associates will assure it. Then I'll be president for life."

Earl's face, normally white as a snow drop, was a fiery red, his speech somewhat slurred.

The girl sobbed, shaking her head back and forth.

Closing the door behind her, Rainey glanced at the table under one of the mirrors next to the wall. A small mound of white powder sat there on yet another mirrored surface .

"Here I come." Earl jumped up on the bed and crawled on all fours until he loomed over the girl.

Her scream pierced Rainey's heart.

Earl laughed. "Oh, I love a girl with spirit. But if you talk, I'll kill you and your family."

Then the girl saw Rainey. Her eyes went wide. "Help! Help!"

Earl turned around, his face an alarming purple. His

eyes bulged. "You again! You were at the back of the banquet."

He scrambled off the bed and lunged toward Rainey.

Who are you?" He reached for her mask, but she stepped back.

She grabbed the Makarov pistol.

"You're the Angel of Death, but you—" He charged her, pinning her arms.

Rainey brought both arms up to break the hold, but the old man was stronger than he looked. He knocked the pistol away.

The girl on the bed struggled to get free.

Rainey brought her knee up between Earl's legs.

He howled and let her go. Then hit Rainey in the jaw. "How dare you? I'm the best president."

Rainey punched him in the face.

He fell back.

Rainey pulled the plastic container out of her pocket and took out the syringe.

"I'm going to rule the world. I'm gon rul furev..." Earl stopped and grabbed his left arm.

Rainey retrieved the pistol and, with her other hand, aimed it at his head. She hoped he'd put his hands up, but he just smiled and said, "Angel of Death. You can't haf me."

Then his face twisted. He let out an agonized cry. He grabbed at the bedpost, but missed. Tried to speak, but only choking sounds came out.

Rainey took a step toward him.

He struggled for breath. Reached a hand toward her, his face pleading for help.

Rainey watched carefully, gun still trained on him.

He looked up into the air and pointed toward the ceiling. A look of wonder came over his face. "Do you see?"

"Yes," Rainey said. "It's real. Go ahead."

Now he reached for the light that only he could see. Earl took a last sharp inhale. His body went rigid and his eyes glazed over. He fell to the floor.

The girl in the bed pushed herself up on an elbow, straining against the handcuffs. They both stared at the heap at the bottom of the bed.

Rainey waited half a minute, gun still pointed.

He didn't move.

She returned the syringe to its case and shoved it into her pocket.

"What happened?" the girl whispered.

Rainey bent down and placed two fingers on Earl's neck.

No pulse.

"He had a heart attack," Rainey answered.

The girl's lip quivered. "I'm sorry."

"I'm not." Rainey took off her mask.

The girl looked surprised.

"Let's get you out of those." Rainey saw a glint of silver on the table beside the cocaine and walked over. Keys to the cuffs. She retrieved them and unhooked the girl's hands.

The girl started to cry in earnest.

Rainey wiped her prints off the keys, then untied the velvet ropes holding her ankles. She took the child in her arms. "It's all right. You can cry now."

She sobbed into Rainey's shoulder for a full minute, then pushed back. Looked up at her. "Thank you for saving me."

"You're welcome. What's your name?"

"Grace," she said in a quavering voice.

Rainey's breath caught. What could be more perfect?

"Grace Jones, ma'am."

"Where are your clothes, Grace?"

She waved her hands toward the bathroom, avoiding looking at Earl's body.

Rainey fetched the pile from the bathroom floor. She grabbed a clean washcloth and ran it under warm water. She washed the mascara off Grace's face, then handed her clothes to her. "Let's get you dressed and out of here."

Grace sorted out her Halloween fairy outfit and started to put it on.

"It's important that nobody knows I was here, Grace," Rainey said.

She paused, eyes wide. "Why?"

"Well, this man was the president and I had a gun. If his people found that out, they might think I came to hurt him. They'd come for me."

"Oh, no," Grace said. "Will they come for me, too?"

"No, sweetie. We'll get you out of here before anyone finds him."

Grace pulled her tights up and stood.

"Shoes?"

"Oh." Grace pushed her feet into ballet slippers that had been discarded beside of the bed.

"Now, I know this is hard, but it's best if you don't tell anyone about me. Not even your parents. I apologize for having to ask."

"My father left. Mother drinks."

"I'm sorry."

"It's OK. I thought I could be a movie star, but—" She shook her head, pushing back sobs.

"You will be amazing no matter what you decide to do. Just look what you survived tonight."

Grace looked up at Rainey, her blue eyes clouded with doubt.

Rainey lifted the girl's chin. "I know it."

"Thank you."

"Do what is in your heart."

Grace nodded.

"Now, let's get you downstairs. Can you walk past Earl?"

She nodded. "He was mean."

"Yes, he was."

Rainey pushed the door open. She used the washcloth to wipe her fingerprints off the doorknob. She'd already wiped the keys. She hadn't touched anything else in the room.

Using the cloth, she picked up the Buddha statue she'd used to break the lock and wiped it clean. She returned it halfway down the hall, her other hand holding fast to Grace's. Sounds of grunting, laughter, and crying drifted from the other rooms as they headed to the stairs.

"This place is awful," Grace said.

"Yes, it is."

Rainey slipped on her mask halfway down the stairs. When they reached the ground floor, they saw the party had thinned out. In the back room, a group of young girls and some boys danced with each other. Two Secret Service agents stood watch. It all looked innocent.

"Thank you. Will I ever see you again?" Grace asked.

"You might not see me, but I'll check on you from time to time."

"Good."

Rainey squeezed her hand. "Now, go on."

Grace straightened up, her head high, and walked into the room.

"Gracie," came a little cry from the buffet room. Two girls ran out and hugged her. "We were worried."

"I escaped," she said.

"Good. This is awful. Let's go down to the pool. Nobody's down there." The three girls walked toward the steps to the outside.

From the hallway, Rainey looked around. Neither of the agents had noticed her. She supposed they were sleepy. She wondered that they hadn't responded to Earl's cries, but then there had been lots of screaming and crying in this house tonight. What a job to have to witness such wrong-doings and be sworn to protect the criminal.

# TWENTY-NINE

Rainey slipped out of the house and walked in the shadows toward the lodge. The lobby felt empty except for a few guests who had fallen asleep on couches, their clothes, or what remained of them, in disheveled condition. She made her way to the women's lounge.

Then remembered Brad.

Opening the door slowly, she peeked in. The sight that greeted her stopped her in her tracks.

Brad had been bent face down over an upholstered bench and shackled to it. The bench was pretty much meant for what was happening—somebody to be bent over it for sex. His feet were spread and secured to the legs of the bench, his butt displayed for any and all. It looked as if it had suffered some damage while she'd been away. His anus and cheeks were bloodied. The spiked dildo lay on the floor nearby.

"Ouch," Rainey muttered.

"Girlfriend." Trixie spread her arms and beckoned

Rainey to her. A handful of other women stood around, apparently joining in the humiliation of Brad.

Trixie pulled Rainey into a muscular hug. "Told you we'd make him wish he was dead."

"Is this the piece of shit that raped you within an inch of your life?" asked a woman Rainey hadn't seen before.

"Uh, yeah," she said.

The woman brandished a cat o' nine tails and flicked Brad's ravished buttock with it. She raised a muffled yelp. "What's the matter? Can't take your own medicine?" She flicked him again.

Rainey looked around the bench at Brad's hanging head. He had a big red ball stuck in his mouth and black straps securing it around his head. He was also wearing some kind of bright red bra to match the gag.

"Holy cow" was all she could say.

"We took pictures," Trixie said. "This piece of shit says a word and we send them to all his friends. Post them on his social media." She kicked the bench, then waved a phone in the air. "Understand, asshole?"

Brad grunted.

"You think this will stop him?" Rainey asked.

"Oh, yeah. Have a look." Trixie scrolled through a plethora of compromising pictures of him being sodomized by several different women with a variety of implements, smiling with an erect penis next to his mouth, next with the penis in his mouth, howling as a woman sat astride his back and whipped him.

"That just might do it," Rainey said.

"I think so. You know these macho types," Trixie said.

"I hope you wore some protection for that one shot."

Trixie threw back her head and laughed. "Always, girlfriend."

Rainey put her hand on Trixie's shoulder. "I can't thank you enough, although the spikes?"

Trixie shrugged. "One of the girls had a rough night."

"I'm leaving," Rainey said. "Can you keep him for another hour?"

Brad tried to talk around the gag.

"If you tell anyone I'm alive, I'll find out and we'll release these pictures," Rainey said. "Do you understand?"

Brad nodded vigorously. Rainey was surprised he still had that much energy.

She went back to her locker, took off her costume, and dressed in her old clothes. She buried the washcloth from Earl's room deep in the bathroom trashcan. Stuck the costume into her bag in case anybody got industrious and looked for DNA evidence. Shouldering her bag, she headed out the door, giving everyone a big wave.

She jogged down the path beside the golf course and headed to the woods. She found the road and continued her jog until she located the footpath to the beach.

When she reached the water, the stars were fading. She ducked under the mangroves and quickly picked her way to the boat. It was still where she'd left it, but now on the strip of sand revealed by low tide. She pushed the boat out, pulled herself aboard and set sail.

## CHAPTER
# THIRTY

O nce the boat rounded the tip of the island, a breeze billowed the sails, and the racing sloop picked up speed. She threw the Makarov pistol overboard, then sat back and relaxed, watching the pink line on the horizon turn golden. The sun rose, round and magnificent.

She'd been spared killing Earl. He'd died from natural causes, if you could call his lifestyle natural. She liked it when things worked out like that.

A spinner dolphin leapt up into the air a few feet off her bow. Then another. Soon a whole pod accompanied her across the water. They stayed with her until she came too close to Miami for their comfort.

She beached the boat just south of the marina on a sandy strip sheltered from view. She scrambled up the beach and walked to a convenience store nearby where she bought a burner phone. Outside, she started walking toward the bus station and dialed Control.

"Gaia's Catering."

"Yes, can I place an order off your special menu?"

"Your ID?"

Rainey punched a series of numbers into the phone.

After a few seconds, the man said, "Please hold."

Another series of clicks and Control answered.

"It's done."

"So I see."

"They found him?"

"It's all over the news. They're reporting a heart attack."

"It was, actually. I didn't have to do a thing, except maybe scare him to death."

"Got away clean?"

"Left two bodies," Rainey said. "Russians. One in Atlanta, the other on the island."

"Were they on your list?"

"One was. The other was trying to kill me." She didn't mention her encounter with her past. She hoped Brad and Grant would keep their mouths shut. If they didn't, well, she could take care of it.

"Excellent. Take a break. We'll be in touch."

She disconnected.

In a couple of blocks, she reached Douglas Street Monorail Station and got back on #42 to the airport.

Once there, she bought a ticket to La Guardia and made her way to the gate. She bought an egg sandwich and hot chai from Starbucks and settled down to wait. The airport had CNN on the monitors.

"President Charles Jefferson Earl died sometime last night in his Florida home of an apparent heart attack. Sources report his health was worse than the report his doctor issued earlier in the year. The doctor recently admitted Earl wrote the report himself, but that the president was secretly being treated for heart disease. Apparently, the stress of the campaign plus the recent impeachment proved to be too much for him.

"Republicans are scrambling to find a replacement for Earl on the ballot. Some report the Vice President will be nominated. Other names are being considered.

"Some speculate Earl's death may generate a sympathy vote. However, polls show Murray ahead by fifteen percent."

Then a retrospective of Earl's life began. Rainey tuned it out.

She punched in Arnold's number. He answered after a few rings.

"Hey, it's me."

"Nice to hear from you. Have you seen the news?"

"I'm looking at it right now."

"Can you believe it? I think the country caught a break."

"Looks like it." Too bad she couldn't tell him.

"What are you up to?"

"Are the leaves still on the trees in New England?"

"I'll see. If not, there's always the Smokey Mountains."

"Let's go celebrate."

Arnold chuckled. "Sounds like a plan."

Want to read Rainey's next adventure? Click here

Join my newsletter to hear about new releases, special

offers, and news. Click here to subscribe. No spam and it's easy to unsubscribe.

Reviews help writers keep writing. Please feel free to leave one!

**Excerpt from *Breached: A Mystic Assassin Novella***

## CHAPTER 31
# EXCERPT FROM BREACHED

Rainey threw her gym bag over her shoulder and headed for the door of the Boston Women's Martial Arts dojo. "Thanks for inviting me," she said to the young woman walking beside her.

"Oh, my Goddess. Thank you for coming. I can't believe you agreed to do it. You're so talented. I had no idea when I saw you doing forms in the park how much you knew." Jessica put her hand over her mouth, her face flushing red, apparently realizing she'd been gushing.

Rainey gave her an easy smile. "It was my pleasure. I love sharing tips, especially with advanced students."

"You really taught us a lot. Can I get you to come back? I didn't even get your phone number." Jessica pushed a strand of sweat-drenched hair behind her ear.

Coming here, teaching in public, was a big risk, but one Rainey was willing to take. Her contract work for a private security group required anonymity. Complete secrecy, in fact. Her own parents thought she was dead. But teaching women to defend themselves was a passion for her.

"I'm not sure how much longer I'll be in town," Rainey

said, "but if it turns out I have the time, I'll drop by and see if you've got an opening."

"We'll make time for you."

Then Rainey spotted him. The man in a brown trilby hat sitting on a bench at the bus stop a block up the street. It looked like Control had a job for her. Rainey squeezed Jessica's shoulder and said, "Gotta run."

Jessica gave her a little wave, then turned back into the lobby. Rainey strolled toward the sidewalk until the young woman disappeared into the dojo, then hurried off. Control's courier caught her eye. He raised his hat and resettled it on his head, their signal, then walked away toward a coffee shop across the street.

Rainey reached the bus stop quickly and took a seat on the bench where the man had been. She leaned back, pretending to be winded. A bus lumbered to a stop and opened its doors with a wheeze. In the bustle of passengers disembarking and others getting on, she leaned down and detached a small envelope beneath the bench.

The weight surprised her. Usually these packages had a thumb drive inside, but she felt a solid rectangular object in this one. Probably one of 7R4C3R's specialty items. Rainey hadn't realized how to pronounce this strange pseudonym until she'd heard Control call his hacker 'Tracer.' She'd never met him in person.

Rainey made her way down a side street in the cooling summer evening, watching for any tails. Seeing nothing, she hit the fob to unlock her used Prius and slid behind the wheel. Placing the envelope in the passenger seat, she pulled into the light traffic and drove the short distance to her apartment in Lower Alston, taking a few false turns along the way. Nobody was following her. Not unless they'd put a team on her that handed her off to each other from time to time.

Rainey always moved to a new town after an assignment. This time she'd picked Boston. University neighborhoods worked best. The undergrads clustered in Alston and the neighborhood was more international, but she hadn't been able to resist the Charles River Reservation. It was the perfect place to run and do her Kajukenbo forms. Nobody gave her a second look. Except Jessica, who'd been going through her own routine early one morning. But Jessica and her organization had checked out. Very low risk.

She maneuvered her Prius into a spot in the street behind her apartment and walked down the sidewalk, swinging her gym bag to appear casual as she scanned the area. Large-leafed sycamores shaded the street, creating shadows for her to move through. The sidewalks were empty, so she slipped into the alley that ran through to her building, walked to the front, and pushed open the door.

The small lobby was empty. A bank of old mailboxes filled one side. A dusty plastic flower arrangement sat in front of a gilded mirror opposite them. Discarded ads littered the table beside the vase. Relieved not to run into any neighbors, she took the steps two at a time to the third floor and then strolled down the hallway to the end to her corner apartment.

The transparent tape at the top of her door was undisturbed. Inside, Rainey did a quick security sweep and found everything as she'd left it. She checked the street below, looking for any unfamiliar cars, but found nothing new. Satisfied, she threw her gym bag into the bedroom and walked into the kitchen, where she placed the envelope onto the small table.

Rainey always observed the same ritual when listening

to a possible assignment. She knew it might be the last quiet time she'd have for a while. She put on the kettle and took out the latest cast iron teapot she'd found in Boomerangs, a thrift shop in Central Square. The type of tea depended on the time of day, so for this evening she chose chamomile. She sprinkled in some rose petals and tossed in a vanilla bean. She picked a blue mug large enough for soup, added a dab of blueberry honey, and waited.

The kettle whistled and she poured water into the pot, leaning over to enjoy the first burst of rose scent. She put the lid on and opened the envelope. Inside was a phone. She switched it on, touched her thumb to the home button, and it unlocked.

*Control must have my fingerprints on file somewhere,* she thought. Not unexpected, but still, she didn't like how much they knew about her.

There was one number stored in the phone's memory.

Before clicking on the entry, she poured tea and took a sip, closing her eyes to savor the unique combination of flavors.

Then she made the call.

"I have a mission, should you choose to accept it," Control said in his well-modulated voice. There was no hint of sarcasm.

Rainey chuckled at his old TV show reference. He always used it. "To what do I owe the pleasure of an actual phone call?"

"It's nice to talk to you as well," he said, pretending offense.

She took another sip of tea and waited.

"Our friends in the agencies need help. They're over-whelmed with leads from the recent coup attempt."

"I can imagine."

Many people who stormed the capitol after the election had been ordinary citizens who'd gone down the rabbit hole of conspiracy theories, following the trail left by bloggers known by single letters and tweets from politicians. Not to mention so-called news channels. These people imagined themselves to be saving their country from corruption. Some claimed late President Earl had been assassinated to clear the way for his challenger to win. Some blamed the opposition party. Others foreign actors.

Only Rainey and the girl she'd rescued from his bedroom knew the truth. She hadn't been forced to use the syringe she'd brought to simulate a natural death. President Earl had died from a heart attack without any assistance from her.

Besides misguided citizens believing in improbable scenarios, who in the group was not hoodwinked? Who was still set on replacing the duly elected officials with their own group of candidates? And how clean was that slate? Earl had been a straight-up Russian asset. No question about it in her mind, although the conspiracy crowd would deny it to the end.

Earl had spouted about a rigged election for months before voting began last November. A number of domestic terrorist groups had coordinated the rebellion after the election, which had been months in the planning. Hell, they'd even printed t-shirts. Members of various law enforcement agencies and the military also participated. The question was in what capacity. It was a lot to sort out.

One thing was clear. It was unlikely everyone had packed up their Winchesters and gone home. What were their future plans? The agencies with their assorted alphabetical acronyms had been weakened by Earl, who'd replaced actual professionals with his cronies. The U.S. defense agencies were overwhelmed, plain and simple.

All this would be enough, but hackers had broken into government computers—agencies responsible for U.S. security, foreign and domestic. They'd left a mess. Files were stolen, corrupted, false information left behind. It was still being sorted out. The hack had made the news, but the FBI had been able to hide how serious the breach was.

"They said we need all hands on deck," Control said.

Rainey snorted. "Are we talking about the military here?"

"A mix, so some."

"Are you sure they didn't say every swinging . . . ?" She left the rest unsaid.

Control chuckled. "All right, they did, but—"

"Then that leaves me out," Rainey said. She took another sip of tea and tried to get comfortable in the vinyl kitchen chair.

"Please, Rainey. We need you. This conspiracy is extensive and, as it turns out, quite complicated."

"But this is not my specialty. I'm not an investigator. Find me a target and I'll go after it."

"You've been trained in all areas of spy craft, my dear."

Rainey bristled at the endearment. "But—"

"You're way better than you think. We know they've got more actions planned. We have to find out how the main actors are connected."

Rainey studied a slight bruise on her hand. Must have been from the training she'd just given.

"We've got to find out how deep this goes," Control said.

She could imagine him straightening his perfectly

groomed hair, which is what he did when he was frustrated. She'd picked up a few of his tells. "Like I said, find me a target."

"Your country needs you," Control said in his low, cultured voice.

Damn the psychologists. They knew her trigger points.

Rainey shook her head in frustration. She'd just settled into her new neighborhood. Just found the perfect teapot. Now she'd have to move again. "What's the mission?"

"7R4C3R will upload it in thirty seconds. Please let me know by tomorrow at noon."

"That's fast," she said. She usually got three days to consult with her spiritual advisors if the target's name was not on her list of approved hits.

"Like I said, the situation is urgent."

Rainey started to end the call, but realized the line was still open. "I can't thank you enough," Control said. "I lost a friend in that attack."

"I'm sorry," she said.

"I'm a professional, but this—this is personal."

He ended the call before she could offer condolences. Control hated sentiment.

Rainey took a sip of her tea, but it was cold. She decided to make a fresh pot. She thought about what Jessica had shared. So many women had similar stories. After the gang rape in Afghanistan, Rainey's time at the Tibetan nunnery had done a lot to heal her trauma. Rising early, chanting with a group of women, some innocent, some also victims of violence, had brought her a peace she had not known existed in this life.

Rainey had almost died in Afghanistan. Four men led by the unit commander Brad Rogers had kidnapped her, taken her out into the desert, staked her out and raped her. One man after another. They choked her, beat her, burned her legs and sides with the muzzles of smoking gun barrels.

In point of fact, they had killed her. She remembered the relief as she flew out of her battered body while a man rutted on top of her, his hands wrapped around her neck, squeezing.

She sailed into a tunnel of light. Light that healed all it touched. Light that was all-encompassing love. Balm. Joy beyond words. The anguish, the fear and rage—it was all gone in an instant.

But before she made it through to the place she wanted to go with every fiber of her being, radiant forms of light barred the way. They handed her a scroll. She'd known what they were asking without any words being exchanged. Remove these people from their current life and send them to us.

For a split second, if there was any time there at all, Rainey wondered why they got to go into this glory and she didn't. But as soon as her glowing fingers closed around the scroll held out to her, she returned with a whoosh and woke in a local hospital with ER workers shouting over her body.

One thing was for sure. Madison Danika Varma was dead. She'd shed her old name and become Rainey.

She finished her second pot of tea and washed out the mug. Then she cleaned the teapot and dried it carefully. She'd take the assignment, but she wasn't going to leave this pot behind. She was tired of having to find new ones every time she moved. She'd ship it to Arnold. After the mission, she would travel to The Oaks. Mull over their last adventure in Peru and what it all meant. Right now, she had a country to save.

. . .

Want to read the rest? Just click here.

# ABOUT THE AUTHOR

Theresa Crater is a bestselling author of award-winning thrillers, fantasy, and paranormal women's fiction. Based in the foothills of Colorado, she travels extensively to write fiction exploring world mythologies, sacred sites, and the universal search for spiritual and human connection.

She has published over thirty works of fiction. She is the author of the Spirit Springs series, the Emerald City Mysteries, and the Power Places and Mystic Assassin thrillers, along with other works.

# Also By

**Theresa Crater**

Emerald City Paranormal Women's Fiction

*Murder, Mystics & Menopause*

*Ghosts, Garters, and Grimoires*

*Crystals, Crooks, and Chaos*

*Whales, Witches, and Wait…What?*

Spirit Springs Paranormal Women's Fiction

*The Crone and the Stolen Orb*

Power Places Series

*Under the Stone Paw*

*Beneath the Hallowed Hill*

*Return of the Grail King*

*Into the City of Light*

*Power Places: The Complete Series*

*Yuletide Tales: Holiday Short Stories*

Mystic Assassin Series

*Assassin Awakens*

*Breached: A Mystic Assassin Novella*

Stand-Alones

*The Star Family*

*Three Awakenings: A Spiritual Memoir*

**Louise Ryder**

*God in a Box*

*School of Hard Knocks*

# ACKNOWLEDGMENTS

As always, special thanks go to Stephen Mehler for his patience and encouragement. Thanks to Virginia King for her help with editing. Special shout out to my Advanced Reader Team for their eagle eyes and helpful suggestions. All the mistakes are mine.